We
Are
Still
Here

We Are Still Here
by Emily Koon

Conium Press
728 NE Killingsworth Ct.
Portland, OR 97211
http://www.coniumreview.com

Published in the United States of America

© 2019 Emily Koon & Conium Press

ISBN 978-1-942387-14-5

Book Editing: James R. Gapinski & Holly Lopez
Cover Image: Tyler Lastovich & Lastly Studios, courtesy of Unsplash
Cover Design & Interior Layout: James R. Gapinski

Individual stories from this collection have been previously published in *The Conium Review*, *Fiddleblack*, *Literary Orphans*, *Paper Darts*, *The Rumpus*, and *Shirley*.

Conium Press holds first print and electronic book rights to this collection. All applicable reprint rights revert to the author. No portion of this publication may be reproduced or stored in any form without the prior consent of the author.

We Are Still Here

stories &
a novella
by Emily Koon

Conium Press

Contents

I.

The People Who Live in the Sears	1
The Ghosts of St. Louis	15
Butterbean	39
We Are Still Here	59
In a Dark Wood	81
Neil deGrasse Tyson	89
Myrtle	93
Lark	105
United Parcel Service	113
Theta Orionis	129
Quantum Tentacles	139
The Water Goblin	155
The Princess	161

II.

Dark Paradise	169

For Minnie, who was with me for all of this.

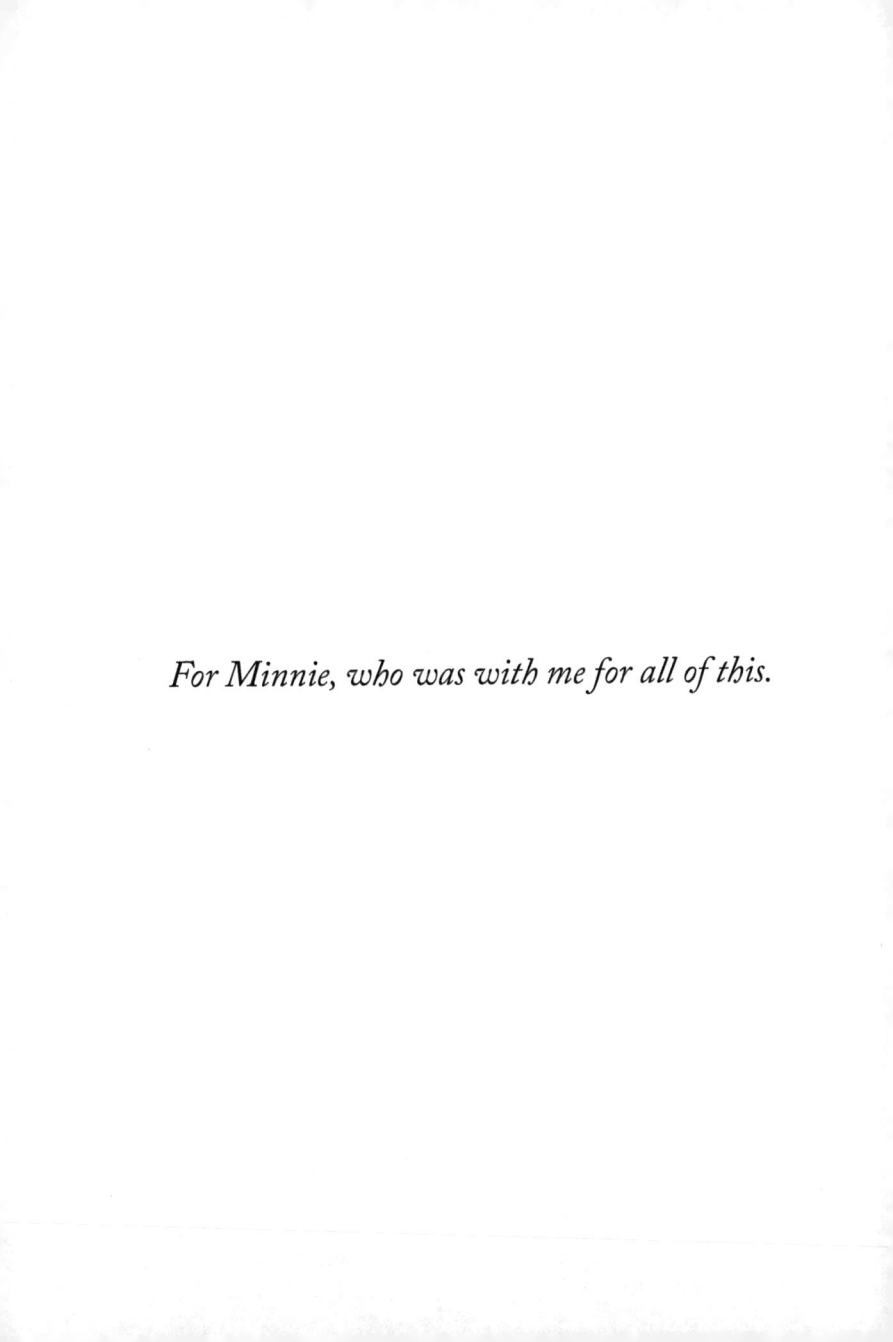

I.

The People Who Live in the Sears

The people who lived in the Sears didn't want to leave. The store's management worried about their bulging red eyes, the way they stalked customers browsing for camouflage pants and adult onesies. Sales were down, which meant the Sears was in danger of closing, which meant the mall would soon have a hole in its south wing. Downhill from there.

Until now, the people in the Sears were tolerated as long as they stayed out of the way. *Don't harass the shoppers, don't mess with the grills. And no sex anywhere on Consolidated Capital Partners property*, not that this mattered. The people who lived in the Sears weren't interested in sex. They were interested in peace, in continuity, and now they were being pushed out.

"To optimize the browsing experience of our guests," the written notice said. Everyone knew this was about the guy who watched the Food Network in his underpants.

The people stared at the store manager with their red bug- eyes and told him what they thought. Life was easy in the Sears. Every morning, they could waddle down to Starbuck's and slurp triple espresso macchiatos until their hearts gave out. No boss on the horn, no hassles. If he thought they'd give that up without a fight, he was tripping.

"Can you guys just get out of here?" the manager said. "The semi-annual sale is coming up, and you losers can't be weirding out the customers."

He'd thought of living in the Sears once too, but the outside never got bad enough. Last month he got the director's cut DVDs of *Battlestar Galactica* and marathoned them with the okay-looking Kirkland's cashier. They made out a little, and it was better than nothing. He thought while kissing her, *This wouldn't be happening if I was living in the Sears.*

The manager was a punk, little more than a kid. The older residents could bully him, but what if they sent in the big guns? The lawyers, the mall cops packing pepper spray. The only things the people in the Sears had for weapons were barbecue tongs. If it came to that, what good were barbecue tongs against a law enforcement infrastructure? Not much.

The people who lived in the Sears formed a big circle around the escalator, hands across America, and realized they had something more powerful than barbecue tongs. They held hands and felt like one giant heart beating together, *thrump thrump thrump*. Loud enough to drown out Celine Dion, the misbehaving children, the beauty-counter ladies baiting customers, the back-to-schoolers trying on Keds. They thrumped so loudly they thought they could silence the whole world.

. . .

Some of the people in the Sears had been there since the '80s, when the mall was built. They got used to the pillow-top mattresses and sectional sofas, the suede espadrilles that made their calves look good, and stayed. The newbies were living out their teenage fantasy of getting locked in the mall overnight. In that fantasy, they tried on all the clothes and fancy dresses they wanted, and what was a fancy dress without a makeover at the Estee Lauder counter? Nothing, that's what. Happiness came after they jumped the display cases and caked foundation on themselves, after they spritzed on Malibu Musk and passed out from the godawful pleasure. Now they could do this every day.

There were dozens, maybe hundreds of people living in the Sears. A few more trickled in every week as they fled failed marriages and the abysmal job market. After the economic upswing, they fled the job opportunities, the compulsion to work. The veterans napped all day. The newbies fretted, not yet lost in the readymade comforts.

"What do you do about food? What's the policy on toilets? Where do you shower?" were the first questions newbies asked, always in that order. Eat, poop, wash.

One of the veterans would pull the newbie out of Small Appliances or Fine China, wherever they were when they realized, *This is it, I live in the Sears now, the mall is my town.* Then the freak-out over logistics. They'd pat the newcomer's arms and give them the rundown, how easy everything would be now, the blissful few choices left to make.

"The food court is open from nine to nine, ten on weekends. The demo Jacuzzi is communal. Pee where you can."

When the veterans first came, they didn't have guides. They had to figure things out for themselves. It was pretty lonely, circling the store all day, pretending to shop. At night they'd climb into the display beds and think about the lives they'd left. Should they go back? Patch things up with Susan? All these years later, they wondered. Who had Susan been? What had she meant to them? There was a vague memory of a drive-in movie theater and Coca-Cola spilled in their laps. *E.T. the Extra-Terrestrial.* They wondered if that was still playing.

. . .

Back-to-school season was a tense time for everybody. The friction between the shoppers and the people who lived in the Sears had a smell like burning rubber.

"Put that *Pirates of the Caribbean* backpack right back where you found it, lady," said the people who lived in the Sears.

The shoppers complained to the manager, or they didn't buy the backpack, Reebok sneakers, patterned tights. Worst case, a stressed-out parent took on the person who lived in the Sears and stood their ground. There were a scary couple of seconds where everybody thought the person who lived in the Sears would lose it. Once in a while, they did.

An urban legend dating back to the 1990s said a mother and her teenage daughter were imprisoned for two days in a camping tent, having bought the last pair of acid-wash jeans with shredded knees. The people who lived in the Sears had just kind of snapped. No one was espousing force, but everyone could see the people who were living in the Sears then had felt oppressed, like wild animals losing their habitat.

"We do not come into your house and take things out of your closet!" the protest signs read that year. The signs this year read, "A Return to Sanity." It was right there on the signs, what the movement was about. They just wanted to send a message: ours, yours. No one meant to burn down the mall.

. . .

The fire started the way all fires start, with a butane camping stove.

Sporting Goods went up like a tinderbox. The explosion blew the revolution's leader backwards into the portrait studio, and when the paramedics pulled her out, her eyebrows and most of her hair were gone. The people who'd lived in the Sears blinked at her in the bright sunlight, which some of them hadn't seen in years. Disoriented, disappointed, they slinked off. She was this injured pink thing no one could see leading a revolt.

Inside the store, the fire raged like it had been waiting for someone to set it. The mall's aging sprinkler system had not been replaced since the 1970s, even though a notice from the Fire Marshall sat on the property manager's desk, warning them of a coming disaster. As if it had been carried around inside each of the people who lived in the Sears until the match was lit near that camp stove's leaking gas canister. The people who lived in the Sears weren't trying to burn the place down, the fire knew this. They were trying to light a small flame, buy the world a Coke, in hopes the people who lived outside the Sears would become sensitive to their plight. But once the fire was loose, it raged.

"I'm a fire, man, that's what we do," it said as it gutted the Lancôme counter.

After the cosmetics counters, the fire took out Juniors with its display of Justin Bieber t-shirts, then Bed and Bath. All that was left was a set of NASA-grade, flame-retardant Wamsutta comforters. At the end of the world, the fire thought, when it was done raging, there would be nothing left but cockroaches and Wamsutta comforters.

After the fire was done with the Sears, it took the rest of the mall. The Kirkland's, the Barnes & Noble, the orthopedic shoe place, each abandoned by its staff and rubbled. The fire's only regret was for the beautiful charred things left in its wake.

"Man, that scrolled wine holder would have looked great in the kitchen."

Then it remembered it was fire. It kept going.

. . .

The fire moved on to the surrounding commercial district, swallowing the Chili's and the wireless phone carrier. The people who worked in these businesses had watched the mall burn, thinking of Mt. Saint Helens erupting on television when they were children. The black and gray smoke was as they remembered. So were their thoughts that somehow this was connected to the end of the world, that all the malls in the country were bursting into flames, just as they'd once thought all the volcanoes in the world were erupting.

The mall was built when they were kids, around the same time Mt. Saint Helens blew its top. Before that, the whole area was open farmland with a dairy. Once, the school took them on a field trip to the dairy. The farmer let them drink fresh cream and pet baby goats wearing crocheted sweaters. They hadn't thought about the goats in years.

. . .

Because the people who'd lived in the Sears didn't have anywhere else to go, they walked east toward the national forest. They couldn't recall much about their old lives, but they thought there'd once been a city on the other side of the forest. If they were remembering right, there was a Sears in it. The city had a skyscraper with a restaurant at the top that slowly turned all day. When your drinks came, you might be looking at the skyline; when your dessert came, you'd be looking at trees.

The fire was ahead of them, but when they turned southeast, taking to the highway, it raged alongside them in the distance. If they turned their heads just right, they didn't have to look at it. Eventually, the fire was only visible as gray smoke above the national forest.

"Who would set a forest on fire?" one of them asked.

An old-timer shook his head. The others worried he wasn't strong enough to make it to the new Sears. "Damn shame, if you ask me," he said. He remembered going to the forest when his children were small. It had trails and swing sets that his pigtailed daughter liked to swing on. "All those memories up in smoke."

"How does a thing like that happen?" the others wanted to know.

It didn't take them long to forget. The moment the road forked and they found the fire could be put out of sight, their thoughts returned to their lives in the Sears. The old-timer was thinking further back than that, to his daughter on the swings again. She'd worn fat bows of orange yarn on each of her pigtails. He couldn't remember what became of her.

• • •

After the fire ravaged the first suburb, it moved on to the rabbit warren of cheap pueblo-style deathtraps in the second. The residents saw the mall fire on television and ignored the warning to evacuate, insisting that suburbs were a zone free of sorrow. This was why they'd moved out here in the first place. Life in the city was suffocating. Other people's dramas played out at the community level—neighbors fighting, passed out drunk in the hallways. The women were followed off the subway by men who pretended to live in the building and then tried to force their way into the apartment. As soon as they had the money saved, they bought this place.

The news said the blaze started in the Sears. The woman who lived in the cul-de-sac unit thought of her sister, who'd been a real firecracker, going out on her own to start an insurance business. They lost touch after it failed. She heard the sister was living in a Sears somewhere, that people did this, that Sears was maybe not a store at all but an assisted living facility for the maladjusted. Or it was a store once, but people took it over.

A handful of people made it out of the suburb. The cul-de-sac woman threw whatever she could grab into a Jazzercise bag, leaving the rubber exercise bands that were already in there for managing stress on the road. She added protein bars and her signed photo of Ed McMahon. She never did win the Publishers Clearing House Sweepstakes, probably wouldn't now that the world was ending and Ed McMahon was dead. Had he died in the flames, or had he been gone for years already? She couldn't remember.

By the time the survivors from the suburb set out, it was hard to tell the places in the town that were on fire from the places that weren't. They saw that the fire had always been raging around them, that they were a part of it. Each of them a single flame lick capable of destroying everything.

. . .

On the third day, the group that had left the Sears approached the valley where the new Sears was rumored to be. Down in the valley, which earlier that day contained their hopes, was an entire town on fire. Its mall was already a smoking crater, along with the Walmart and Church's Chicken and concentric circles of craftsman houses. The skyscraper with the rotating restaurant was still standing, but one side of it was being eaten away by the fire, which hated to destroy a unique piece of architecture like that. From their cliff, the people who'd lived in the Sears could see the fire extended to the horizon in every direction. They couldn't go around it.

"Perhaps we've made a wrong turn somewhere," they said. "This can't be it. It's on fire."

"This has to be it. This is where the Sears *is*," one of them said. She emphasized *is* because Sears *was*, and nothing, not a fire or the end of the world or corporate bankruptcy, could change what was an undeniable fact of being.

By now their pack had grown. People escaping the burning suburbs on foot folded into their ranks: the families, the woman who kept taking exercise bands out to perform fly presses, the man who wouldn't stop talking about goats in sweaters, who was certain this same fire was happening everywhere, in every town in America, maybe the world.

They headed back up the cliff, a gang of hundreds,

thousands, slowed by the old-timer, who they'd hoped to lose by now. The group was so big, so slow, so mad at the old-timer that at first they didn't notice the flames inching up the hill behind them. When they finally smelled the burned flesh of the stragglers, including (thank God), the old-timer, the ones who were able to ran—up the cliff, back to the highway, toward any town that wasn't burning, toward whatever Sears in whatever part of the country was still left standing to welcome them.

The Ghosts of St. Louis

The guy on the news says the Atlantic and Pacific are one ocean now. It's been like that for a while, just no one's said. We've lost California, Florida, all the original Thirteen Colonies. There's no Gulf Coast anymore because there isn't a gulf. There's just this bit in the middle of the country. We're being swallowed up by something called the Pangeal Sea.

"Woo wee, Rayanne, it's hot. I'm sweating like a whore in church," Bon Bon says. Bon Bon's my cousin. She's living with us until Aunt Kitty gets out of the iron lung. On Sundays I take the tram into town with her so she can sit next to the lung and tell her mom what-all happened during the week. After the

Bon Bon update, one of us wipes Aunt Kitty's face off of tears, and she asks how things are going with me. I try to say something that will cheer her up or at least give her something to think about, lying there all day. This week it's the Atlantic and Pacific merging, how they reached out their fingers until some of them touched and made a new thing.

"Well, shoot, the world just keeps on turning while I'm in this thing," Aunt Kitty says. She says that whatever I say. The continent shrinking, the price of genSorgh® going through the roof. Sometimes I think she doesn't really listen to what we say on account of the iron lung. It's her whole world. If that was my life, I wouldn't pay attention to stuff either.

• • •

On Friday, school is closed because we're at seven on the Air Quality Index. One being clean sweet air you could sleep outside in and ten being total lockdown. Me and Bon Bon are still in our pajamas when my mom leaves for work. She's one of the productivity inspectors that walk the floors at the genSorgh facility. Without her, all that brown fluff would never make it from the little chutes dangling over the belt into boxes of cereal, cooking flour and baby ration. There would be a lot of waste. Mom says the job is shitty but it could be worse. She could still be on the lines, working the levers on the chutes till her hands cramp.

"Don't go outside or shoplift at the commissary or set anything on fire," Mom says inside her respirator. It covers her nose and mouth and makes her sound like a robot that's given up on becoming human.

We won't do any of that because of how bad it smells outside, like hot garbage and melted plastic. Nobody wants to smell that. We stay inside all day in the clean recycled air that doesn't make our lungs hurt. We watch news reports and jump on the couch because we can. We're young, we're the future of this planet, if it has one.

"Renewed unrest in the border states of the Caucasus this week. Skirmishes reported along the neutral zone."

The guy on the news talks in this bored news-guy voice kind of like my mom's respirator voice, like he's given up, too. He's read the same report a hundred times. The anarchies in Europe fighting over the wind turbines, blowing up their best chance for survival. Things are pretty bad over there, way worse than here.

I know what anarchy is, what that means. At town hall meetings, the Councilors will sometimes talk about the damage not having laws over there has done to world peace. How lucky we are to have laws and people working together and Councilors. A system keeping all of us alive. I guess they're right. I guess things could be a lot worse.

"There's nothing on," Bon Bon says.

She says it out of habit, because there's never much on except news reports. When I was a little kid, there were still cartoons and game shows and stuff. You could save up your recreation rations and buy space on the settlement's public access channel. We had this one show called *Cookin' with Shirl*. Our lunch lady Miss Mabel went on and showed how she makes fiestada. People liked it because it wasn't bad news or air quality reports. Like, the world couldn't be falling apart if a lady was on TV making fiestada. *Now, we want this hamburger ground real fine.*

Switching channels, I find a celebrity gossip show with a breaking news feed going. The camera zooms in on Ariel Waxwing Saint, the most famous folk singer in the world, being loaded into an ambulance. The headline flashes SAINT PROTEST ENDS, SINGER RUSHED TO SANTA FE MEDICOMP. The subhead flashes SEPARATION FROM TUTTLEMORE CONFIRMED BY SOURCES CLOSE TO THE SINGER. The subhead of that flashes WILL HE RUSH TO HER SICKBED???

For the last six months Ariel Waxwing's been living

in a redwood in the North American Tree Sanctuary. The tree's called Cheyenne, the last redwood in the world, and she's about as famous as Ariel Waxwing. Some dicks in the Energy Procurement Bureau want to chop all the sanctuary trees down for fuel, including Cheyenne, and Ariel's said they'll have to go through her to do it.

"The protest wasn't going good to start with," Bon Bon says because she keeps up with this stuff. "Ariel Waxwing was starting to look sick. Then that jerk goes and has divorce papers sent right up Cheyenne."

The jerk is Rowan Tuttlemore, celebrity oceanographer. He's on the TV all the time saying end-of-the-world type stuff, like if we don't intervene now, it may be too late. When everybody can see it's too late. He laces his fingers together and bounces them up and down to show that what will save us is more cooperation, less infighting. The social fabric and whatnot. Tuttlemore came up with the name Pangeal Sea for the new ocean that's swallowing us. People thought that was so smart they gave him a call-in show.

Famous-people breakups aren't my thing, though. "Who cares?" I ask. "You're dead inside, Rayanne," Bon Bon says. She heard that expression a couple weeks ago and now she trots it out every chance she gets.

According to the reporter, the protest ended when

Ariel Waxwing passed out from a hunger strike and paramedics hauled her down from Cheyenne. When the camera zooms in on her again, weak and shrunk up on a fluid drip, I shut the tube off. I don't want Bon Bon getting wound up.

A couple weeks ago, they moved Aunt Kitty into a special quarantine ward where we can't visit. Bon Bon's handling it about like you'd think. The guidance counselor at school hauled Mom in about it. Mom told her she's a single mom and a single aunt and held up her chapped hands to show that she's doing the best she can with what she has, which is nothing.

The counselor sighed because it's like that with all the parents. Her job is to tell people stuff they can't do anything about.

Bon Bon wonders out loud if Ariel Waxwing Saint always wanted to be an activist, or a folk singer. If the reporter and paramedics always wanted to be a reporter and paramedics. Were these their dreams as little kids or did they just take the first job that came along?

"I'm going to be a scientist when I graduate out of that school, just like Rowan Tuttlemore," I say.

I won't study whales and sponges and stuff, though, or waste time getting married to folk singers. I thought up this thing called Gunko3000, basically a big old vacuum cleaner that pulls all the crud out of the air and the ocean, the chlorofluorocarbons and the gray sludge and the things everybody these days feels terrible about. I'm gonna build that.

"I'm going to be an activist like Ariel Waxwing Saint," Bon Bon says, leaping into the air. She lands wrong and hits her head on the coffee table and I have to put iodine on her scalp. It runs down her face and stains it with sick mustard-yellow tears, like how the sky looks today.

• • •

The sky is the color of the chalky orange sherbet they sell at the commissary. Not as angry as it was yesterday, when the AQI was a six. Then it was the color of egg yolk. Today it's a five, as low as it ever gets, so they reopen school.

On the rec field, me and Bon Bon hang out on the fringes like always. Miss Nelson tried to have class like normal, but what she didn't know was we'd all made this silent pact to be jerks all day. She couldn't keep a single butt in a seat. I almost feel sorry for her, trying to educate us on a day like this.

I wonder what Miss Nelson is when she's not teaching. Does she just kind of go hollow on the inside and gradually fade to nothing? Does she sit up all night and stare at the wall, waiting to turn into a teacher again in the morning? Nobody knows where her pod is. There's a rumor she sleeps on the cot in the quiet room.

"Oh, God, here comes Dickie again," Bon Bon says.

Not everybody's having a good time during the free period. That's because Dickie Farkus is running around snapping the girls' training bra straps, his mission in life. Bon Bon stands with her back to the outside wall of the gymnacafetorium wishing she didn't have boobs. She doesn't need to worry because I'm prepared to pound Dickie. Done it before. Bon Bon's family. One day after I've grown boobs too, we'll be all each other's got.

"This is stupid. Why did they even have school today?" Bon Bon says.

"I guess they don't know what else to do with us."

We're supposed to be identifying rocks, but nobody is. Miss Nelson handed us geology worksheets on our way out and was all, "just because we're getting an extra rec period doesn't mean we can't learn something." The worksheets are blowing around the playground like ghosts trying to get back in their bodies.

"Go toward the light!" I say, running after the papers, waving my arms at them.

I'm trying to cheer Bon Bon up. The last few days, she's been looking sad the way she does right before she picks all the skin off her lips till they're raw hamburger. After the lip picking comes not brushing her hair or taking showers. I don't even want to think about what comes after that.

It's taken me a few years to work it out, but now I know that Bon Bon's moods and the color of the sky have something to do with each other. One time in elementary school the AQI stayed at nine for three straight days, and she pulled her hair out strand by strand. I had to go behind her with a broom and a dustpan. Not really, but still. The sky was a burnt orange color, and Bon Bon's scalp showed through her hair, and we knew, even though we were little kids, what color the clouds are when the world can just barely keep us alive.

The sky today is really best-case scenario, the most we can hope for. Bon Bon picks at her lip, wondering how a sherbet sky and sherbet air that tastes like chalk going down are supposed to be enough. I know she's wondering that because I'm wondering that. Everybody out here that isn't popping bra straps is wondering that.

There are books in the school library showing orange skies before the war—sunsets, not sick air. Back in those days, most of the really bad stuff was still ahead of them, the sea levels rising, countries splitting in two over who would lead them out of hell. In North America, the sky lighting up tangerine coast to coast, an orange daylight that lasted three weeks. They tell us in school that we're supposed to be grateful we didn't have to live through those days. What those people went through, the ones that survived.

We shuffle around the dirt ground of the quad for a while, me guarding Bon Bon's back from Dickie, both of us kicking rocks we're supposed to be logging on our worksheets. We wait for Miss Nelson to sit down with the book she brought out in her armpit. *Nineteen Eighty-Four*, by George Orwell. A little slice of time opening up.

"Let's go look at the fence," I say.

• • •

The fence is on the other side of some woods separating the civilian part of the settlement from everything else. It's a monster, as fences go. The Council built it on top of the dam ten years ago when people started breaking into the hydroelectric plant to steal juice for their phones and HAM radios. If not for the hydro dam, we'd be in the dark. If not for the hydro dam, we'd slide right into the Pangeal Sea.

"I'm gonna look at the skyline again," Bon Bon says, and she's up the fence like a squirrel.

I don't really want to climb the fence, even though coming out here was my idea. But Bon Bon's been in this funk, and I'll do just about anything to make her feel better. When we've been climbing for about five minutes, my arms start to shake. I loop them through the chinks and hug myself, thinking what my neck will look like with a right angle in it when I fall off this thing. Bon Bon zips up the fence. She isn't afraid of anything except orange skies. She's going to be an activist, chaining herself to trees and other things that need saving.

"I can see it," she says.

About a quarter of the way up the fence, you can see what the world used to look like, before it fell apart. I suck it up and climb to where Bon Bon's stopped, and there it is, just below the surface of the gray water, a grid of dark rectangles and domes. A city that used to be called St. Louis.

Hundreds of years ago, when the Mississippi River started flooding the land along its path south of here, they built a dam. I wrote a report on it last year. For years, as far as the people of St. Louis knew, it held back the end of the world. Then there was a little spark deep in the earth a hundred miles south. A fireball in the continent's gut. Highways moved like ocean waves. Trucks bounced around like toys. There was a sound like thunder right before, or if you asked some people it was like heavy hail falling, or just a low roar that meant they should have run. I guess the couple of minutes right before you kick sounds different to everybody. When I go, it'll be like a herd of stallions running across the prairie. What it would sound like if there were any stallions anywhere, if prairies were still a thing.

While people were busy pulling bodies from the rubble of St. Louis, the cracks in the dam spread like roots, and the city was an underwater ghost town in a few weeks. There are photos in the Citizens' History Museum of what the city looked like right after the flood. The water was lower, and clear enough that you could see everything that was lost.

"The water looks gross today. I can't see anything," Bon Bon says.

"It always looks gross."

"Last time I could see all the way down to the streets. The lights in the carnival came on and there were spirits riding the Ferris wheel. Just going around and around and around and never getting off."

She can see dead people now, I guess. Like, there's this whole world going on right beside us that most people can't see. We're separated from it by invisible glass, and occasionally a shriveled gray arm will reach across the void and make contact. If I was a ghost, I wouldn't want nothing to do with the world that killed me.

"All that's down there is the remains of people who were too sick or old or hurt to make it out in time." I say.

Bon Bon is a believer, one of the people who think what's down there can be saved. They're still caught up in the story of St. Louis. Someday it'll rise out of the flood waters and not be this rotten city anymore. We'll all move into the houses and our parents will pack into the high-rise corporate centers and sell computer chips and real estate and the world will start over again.

"Think about it," I say. "You drowned in a big flood, you lost everything. You don't know what happened to all the people you knew. You're a ghost. First thing you're gonna do is ride a Ferris wheel?"

She climbs, puts some space between me and her. She doesn't want me to follow her. Or talk to her, or anything. Lip skin and hair, turning the apartment into a bird nest.

"It's depressing hanging out with you sometimes, Ray Ray."

. . .

The quake that flooded St. Louis is still happening. Aftershocks, humming way down deep. Every hundred years or so, another spark works its way to the surface, and the people living around here have to start over. It makes this one of the most dangerous places on earth to be, but we stay. There's not a lot else to choose from.

I've never climbed this high, but Bon Bon has plenty of times. She went halfway to the top on a dare once, claimed she could see clear to Arcadia, thirty miles away. I don't know if she was yanking my chain or not. All I know is from here I can see all the way across the huge bay that used to be the river basin. Water all the way to the horizon, no other cities or people. We could be all that's left and who'd know? I look for the spot where the tower my old man was working in collapsed, but Bon Bon's right. Except for that top slice of St. Louis, there's nothing to see.

• • •

Me and Bon Bon were little kids when the government started building the new dam. My mom won't talk about it, but Bon Bon heard it from Aunt Kitty. My old man and his crew were working without harnesses when the rumbles started. The tower was almost finished. After the boss called everybody down, those six guys and Joelle Dickerson, better known as Joelle the Harelip, stayed to screw on a few last rivets. They were saving themselves the long, slow trip up and down in harnesses the next day.

It was a bad time. Bon Bon's old man had just got his head blown off by a busted steam pipe at the genSorgh factory. Then Aunt Kitty's lungs went bad on account of the orange air from the orange war, and Bon Bon moved in with us. Even though it was awful for everybody, I liked having somebody to sleep with, to grab onto when I had that dream about our whole town falling into the ocean. I wouldn't tell Bon Bon this, but now that we're older I still like sharing a bed with her. On the nights when I feel myself falling, I don't have to go far to find somebody to hold.

• • •

Poking up over the horizon is the New Tower, a vertical rectangle with a silver pyramid on top. "Rising from the ruins of its predecessor," the dedication plaque reads. Men with sniper rifles are hiding inside it. Bon Bon waves. She knows they won't shoot at kids.

"Hi, guys." She gives a last wave, and when nobody comes out with a bullhorn to run us off, we get on with the blessing.

"Peace go with you. Go in peace," we say. "Peace be

your today and all your tomorrows."

In our settlement, this is what you say when someone dies or leaves in search of a better life or just disappears. The Chief Councilor said the whole blessing at the opening of the New Tower last year, after they riveted on the metal plaque with all the names of the dead on it and read them all off. The blessing is forty-seven stanzas long. We had to memorize it all in Community Hygiene class, so if we're ever stuck at the bottom of a well or anarchists take out the power grids we'll have something to mumble into the dark. *The long dark has ended. Our linked elbows are Community. Our linked arms are the Future.*

Today we just say the first part of the blessing, the important part. It's kind of corny, like knocking on wood, but we're afraid not to say it. Like, maybe if we don't a spell will break and the people under the water won't ever get out of there.

I scan the ancient skyline for signs of life. There's a dark shadow moving past the arch. A shark, maybe even a manta ray. People have started claiming to see weird things in the water. Nobody wants to think stuff like that could be this far in yet, the sharks and rays and jellyfish and stuff. Whatever the thing is, it circles the arch and moves back toward the city and eventually disappears into it. After it's gone, the water is still and quiet. Not a creature stirring, even a mouse.

"Did you see that? What the hell was it?" Bon Bon says.

"Probably a school of electric eels," I say.

"I'm pretty sure those are extinct."

"Look it up," I shrug, even though from where she is she can't see me.

It's weird to think a whole society lived down there once. Some of them might still be in their houses. Every couple of years, a person with a dreamy look in their eye stands up at a town hall meeting and asks why we don't try to take back the city. Build an oxygenated dome, pump the water out and start over. An iron lung big enough to fit all of us. Once in a blue moon someone mechanical will draw it out on paper. They'll unroll the paper and say, *look, it's this easy, we already have the tools.* The papers and sometimes the person who draws them will disappear.

I can feel Bon Bon up there stewing at me. It's been building all day, this feeling that she's sick of me. We spend too much time together, the guidance counselor told Mom that. She said Bon Bon needs other friends and I need other friends. It's always been the two of us, against the Dickie Farkuses and the collapsing towers of the world. I guess I'm a little sick of her, too, even though I know the only reason she came out here was so I wouldn't have to go by myself. It's why I go on the tram with her every Sunday. I like Aunt Kitty, but she's Bon Bon's mom. I'm thinking about my old man clawing at dirty water when I feel Bon Bon moving again. We're already up high enough that if one of us fell, that would be it. I think about the guy who committed suicide off the top of the genSorgh grain elevator a few years back, how his leg was bent in a V shape in the wrong direction. His face has my face on it. My face has Bon Bon's face on it.

"Yo, Bon, I don't think we should go any higher," I yell up.

"*We* don't have to. We can go back down if we're scared," she says.

Each of my heartbeats is a foot placed in another chink in the fence. She's climbing too fast, almost to the halfway point. One wrong move, and she'll come skinning down the fence. Most of me wants to leave her there, save my own neck. My arms are shaking from holding onto the fence so long. I should probably climb down before they give out, but without me telling them to, my feet find the other chinks above me. I know Bon Bon's crossed the midpoint of the fence by now. The highest anybody's ever gone. I'm almost sorry nobody else is here to see it, and then I remember the man from the genSorgh factory, that red chunk of his skull sitting next to his body like a hunk of pomegranate.

St. Louis is a smudge in the water below me. Now I can see the other side of the bay we're in, that it's not closed off like I thought. There's high ground beyond it and a kind of estuary in the middle. The factories and residential compounds and security towers of Arcadia spiking over the new horizon.

"Wow, Bon, you see that?" I say. It's a dumb question because she's been this far up before.

"Yeah, Ray, we gotta go," she says. "Now."

The fence rattles as Bon Bon changes directions, climbing down toward me like the devil's on her tail. Then I see the red light flash on the North Tower's top spike, the navy-suited bodies on the watchtower waving sticks I know are rifles.

"Move along, citizens," the voice from the bullhorn says. The voice is followed by a rifle crack, a warning shot fired into the air. Bon Bon thinks they're firing at us.

"Haul ass," she says, and we do.

. . .

Going down, I keep my eyes on the city. Try to think of anything other than falling off the fence. I think of the story Miss Nelson told us about Atlantis. The people who lived there were an advanced people, real smarties. They had aqueducts and toilets and everything. They all looked around and said *Dang, what a future we built for ourselves*, and then just like that it was gone. The whole island underwater. They didn't feel smart then. All those lives, all that possibility. If people from another island rode by in a boat, they'd never have known the Atlanteans existed.

Bon Bon makes it to the ground a minute or so before me. "Hurry up, Ray Ray, they got guns and stuff."

When I'm a couple of Ray Ray lengths from the bottom, the gun cracks again. It echoes off the fence, the face of the dam, anything solid around the bay, sending the warning back to me again and again. This is not a place for children. This is not a place for any civilized person. I hold my breath and listen for stallions in the distance. Their hooves beat out a message. *Get off that fence, get off that fence*, so I jump.

. . .

With the pain shooting from my left foot all the way up my leg, I can't get up or run or do any of the stuff Bon Bon yells at me to do. A broken ankle, with my luck. When Bon Bon notices the bulge where my ankle juts out funny, she presses her fingers into the soft place under the ankle bone. Something gives. A little piece of bone or cartilage or whatever shifts a millimeter. I let loose a string of cusses I did not know were inside me. Somehow I don't pass out.

"Holy turkey titties."

"Sorry," she says. "It's swole up bad."

"You think?"

More than an hour later, we hobble out of the woods and back into the civilian side of the complex, me using Bon Bon as a crutch. The longer we go without getting shot, the more we worry about how long we've been gone, what Miss Nelson will do to us when we get back to class. How skinned alive we are when we get home.

"We got a week of caf duty with Miss Mabel, easy," I say.

"Well, I don't want to peel no potatoes."

"I don't want to make no fiestada."

"Sorry, Ray Ray, but we gotta pick up the pace."

She hunches down so I can climb on piggyback, even though I'm bigger than she is, and runs us both back into the school yard. She moves faster than I've ever seen her move. Faster than she'd run if Ariel Waxwing Saint was signing autographs. Faster than when she thought we were getting shot at.

• • •

We think we're so smart, just sneak into our seats without anybody noticing. Figure the ankle out later. It's 2:30. Fractions. Miss Nelson will have her back turned writing on the board, and we can scoot in, play dumb. *I don't know what you're talking about, Miss Nelson, we've been there the whole time.* But when we get back, it's just Miss Nelson sitting alone in the classroom, smoothing out a stack of worksheet souls she's saved from the playground. We don't waste paper or anything here.

"Where on earth have you two been? Why are you walking like that, Rayanne?" she says. She knows exactly where we've been, but she can't bust us like she wants to. Anybody can see she's let the rest of the class go early. Dickie could have snapped half the bras in the settlement by now. "I'd call both your mothers, but they've got enough on their minds."

This is supposed make us feel bad, and it does. We take our demerit slips and mumble how sorry we are, which we kind of are but kind of aren't because if we don't ever climb the fence then it's just a bunch of stories that can't possibly be true. We couldn't see the city glittering under water that shouldn't be there. Taken over by weird sea creatures casting dark shadows, calling dibs on the city. *This is ours now.* The Ferris wheel lit up in colored lights and turning under the gray water. We wouldn't see the ghosts of St. Louis, of my father and his crewmates. People who should have made it. Their eyes are black with silt, their hair streaming in the current. They think of the lives they might still be living if they'd been more careful. Taken safe work that didn't mean anything. If they'd just grabbed the people they loved and ran. They go through the motions of their old lives, finding their hearts aren't in it because their hearts have stopped. They've lost their voices but still mouth at us with blue lips as if to say *please try and survive, please, please, please try to make it.*

Butterbean

When the baby appeared on her mantel shelf, singing its heart out and kicking its legs, Pamela thought she was having one of her nightmares.

The one where the baby comes out a full-grown adult and splits her body open.

The one where it's the consistency of gelatin, its insides visible. The red gummy heart beats bravely, the pink gummy lungs rising and falling, bringing Pamela in and out like the tides. The doctor says, "Nothing to worry about, he's just gummy."

But she did worry. More than anything else, her dreams were about the vague sense of dread she carried with her always, the sense that doom was just around the corner.

The child on her mantel shelf wasn't gummy or a dream. He looked like a carnival kewpie with a lick of yellow hair on his head., otherwise baldheaded. She called him Butterbean.

"Ooh wee oooh wee oh," Butterbean sang night and day. When his voice gave out, he whistled.

"Oh, Butterbean, you unexpected gift," Pamela said.

"Ooh ee oh ee oh woo," he sang for the joy of life, babbling in that weird alien language of children just learning to speak.

• • •

Before Butterbean became hers, Pamela tried to give him back. Return the gift.

"Babies don't just show up on people's mantels," said the police officer who took her call.

Pamela knew babies didn't just turn up like that, but this wasn't a hallucination, a fabrication of events. She explained how for ten years she'd had an important job doing public relations for Organic Aromatics, the country's number one maker of natural body products. Balms and whatnot, nothing with harsh chemicals. The factory reminded her of Willy Wonka, with giant mixers turning twenty-four hours a day and people scurrying in white jumpsuits like Oompa Loompas, pouring oils and butters into the pots. Every now and then, someone found an Oompa Loompa toe in their hair wash, and she wrote press releases that made them forget. *The toe was reattached without loss of motor function.* There were a lot of accidents, lots of strange things happening among the vats, so she was busy. She worked her will on the will of others, shifting them into alternate dimensions where facts were different, making changes to the timeline. Her press releases were like magic spells.

Sometimes she thought of her own life in terms of a press release heading. *Local woman gets everything she ever wanted.* What she wrote had a way of coming to be.

The police officer transferred to her Behavioral Health, and they told her the same thing: babies didn't appear out of thin air. Would she mind coming in for a psychiatric screening?

"I would mind that very much," she said and then hung up the phone.

After that, Butterbean was hers. She rocked him in the silver light of late night television, before work, whenever he'd let her. Through David Letterman, Jon Stewart, Jerry Springer, the Home Shopping Network, reruns of *Mary Tyler Moore* and *The Gong Show*. He wouldn't be hers forever. He'd go off to college one day, join a fraternity, register with the Green Party. He might slip out of her hands and back into the fold in space he tumbled out of.

Butterbean went along with the rocking. If he had his druthers, he'd be sitting on the mantel shelf, singing his nonsense, but having someone to love him wasn't bad. He hadn't come there to be her baby, but he understood that letting the woman rock him was a small price to pay for singing his song.

. . .

When she was a little girl one Christmas, Pamela got one of those battery-operated dolls that crawl and say *Mama*. Its name was Baby Get Up and Go, and if she pressed a button on its belly it scooted around the room. It was programmed to occasionally fall down so she'd have to comfort it like a real baby. Pamela had circled it in the Sears catalog, the only thing she wanted that year, but once she had it it troubled her. It had that terrible tickle laugh all dolls have, like an unclean spirit had been imprisoned in its voice box. But unlike regular dolls, this one laughed of its own free will, in the middle of the night, in rooms by itself. After that bad babysitter Kirsten let her watch

Child's Play, Pamela became sure it would come to life and attack her. She decided not to sit around waiting for the axe to drop. One day she took Baby Get Up and Go out to the sidewalk and sent it waddling down the street, out of her life.

. . .

Pamela's downstairs neighbor Felix could see Butterbean, too.

The night he found out about Butterbean, Felix dropped by her apartment, fancying a bite at the Persian place.

"Been thinking about kabobs all day," he said.

This was a lie. He was thinking about her, the night of that awful *Battlestar Galactica* marathon when she ripped his heart out. Until three months ago, they were a sort-of couple, occasionally going out to dinner and movies and once an interpretive dance performance. The dancers had been naked except for a layer of turquoise paint, with puffs of turquoise hair covering their privates.

During the ill-fated marathon, which was Felix's idea, Pamela admitted to herself that he was nice but kind of a dork. She didn't feel bad. He'd find someone else eventually. She only wished for a little more space, a city block at least, between her and Felix. But he couldn't let her go, which was why every day he found some small excuse to make contact with her. There were drop-ins, texts about kabobs, weather, anything he could string between them into a love affair.

Now Felix had a big excuse to knock on her door, something real to string between them. He tied one end to himself and the other to her, like patio lights.

"If we could just figure out how Butterbean got here. That's the biggest mystery of all, his materialization," Felix said, materializing closer to Pamela on the sofa. "Poor thing. Does he understand what we say to him?"

Pamela didn't like talking about where Butterbean came from. She knew if you pulled long enough on a thread it eventually led you back to its source. She didn't want to go asking questions that would unravel the whole thing. Birth mothers, missing persons. And anyone could see there was a metaphysical reason for Butterbean's presence. Like the police officer said, babies didn't just appear on mantels.

"Maybe I could talk to him in German," Felix said. His grandparents immigrated from Berlin in the thirties, which was how he knew a little.

"I don't think the language is the issue. Butterbean is a baby."

Felix scooted closer and put his arms around her. She felt hungry, but not for him.

"You're a baby. You're my baby," he said. His lips gathered into a kiss and came at her. They filled Pamela's apartment.

His hand went under the back of her shirt, going for her bra clasp, but before he could unhook it, Pamela remembered. Butterbean needed his bottle. It was an old trick from when they dated. He'd go at her bra, and some urgent need or responsibility would surface. The dishwasher needed starting, the kitchen floor had a scum on it that had to be dealt with right then. It worked like a charm. Felix dematerialized from her cushion.

Local woman extricates self from Felix Gruber.

In the six months since Butterbean appeared, Felix had floated a dozen wild theories about him. He checked him for a hidden battery pack, making sure he wasn't a lifelike toy. He made jokes about Butterbean being a baby Cylon. *There are many copies, and Butterbean has a plan.* Lately, the mystery was deepening because Butterbean wasn't growing like other babies. He should have been more than a year old, but he wasn't walking, putting little sentences together, anything.

Felix worked Butterbean's lack of development into the equation.

"He must have a genetic disorder that's keeping him from aging on the traditional trajectory. It must be why his birth family rejected him."

"You think he's Benjamin Buttoning," Pamela said.

"It's the only thing that fits."

The fact that Butterbean could sit on the mantel shelf all day without falling off, even while Pamela was at work, seemed like proof of this. What real nine-month-old could you leave in the house alone all day, as Pamela did? What baby didn't grow, Felix insisted, if there wasn't a full-grown adult living inside it?

"That doesn't prove anything," Pamela said. She was thinking of the dream where her baby comes out a college student.

"I read an article this morning that said scientists figured out how to reverse the aging process in mice. They mucked around with the chromosomes. Elderly mice ended up with the bones and muscles and skin of newborns. Pamela, Butterbean could be a hundred years old."

Butterbean wasn't a lab experiment gone wrong, a cuddly Frankenstein with a lick of yellow hair. Experiments like what Felix was talking about always went haywire, Pamela knew.

"Didn't you read *Flowers for Algernon* in high school?"

she called in from the kitchen, where she filled bottle after bottle with formula.

"That was a fiction, Pamela. This is real life," Felix said, sweeping her concerns under the living room rug. "What if he's regressing slowly, and he keeps getting younger until he's just an egg?"

Until he didn't exist. Pamela thought of Butterbean growing smaller and smaller, one day a three-month-old, a newborn, finally reverting to a fetal state. He would curl into a bean befitting his name, arms and legs withdrawn into buds. Then a round mass of pearly cells vibrating with potential, then nothing. Felix kept talking about chromosomes, his voice high and strained, some panic in it. Pamela let the noise recede until Felix was a *rawr-rawr-rawr* at the edge of her hearing, like a brown bear pawing its way into a beehive. *Let me in let me in let me in.*

. . .

When Pamela's sister was born, their parents named her Denise, but Pamela wanted to call her She-ra. Princess of Power. Like the doll from the Sears catalog, her sister came out different than she'd thought. Fragile and spastic, the skin on her eyelids and nostril arches almost see-through. A lace of fine veins ran under all her surfaces.

Pamela thought if she stared at Denise long enough she could see through her to the red gummy heart beating in her chest.

One day, she sneaked into the nursery and got Denise out of the crib. Pamela misjudged the baby's weight and fell backwards onto the carpet, clutching for dear life the weird little sister who'd thrown off the balance in the house. Her parents were like children themselves, doing things Pamela didn't understand. Buying a new car when the old one was fine. Did money grow on trees? She worried they didn't know what they were doing, bringing more kids into the world, and when their incompetence came to light she'd have to take care of Denise.

Denise didn't hit her head or anything—nothing bad happened, not then with Pamela holding her, not later in Denise's life that she could ever see—but she cried anyway.

"Shut up, Denise," Pamela said.

"Don't tell Denise to shut up," her father said as he and their mother ran in.

"And you shouldn't pick her up without help. Denise is not a doll," her mother said.

Pamela had plenty of those in her room. The one from Sears must have been halfway to California by then. She wondered. If she put Denise out on the sidewalk, how far would she get?

. . .

All Christmas Day, Pamela's family tried to unspool the truth about Butterbean. They stared at him, then at Pamela, then back at Butterbean, as though the answers would be read in their skins. When this failed, the questions came. How long was the foster arrangement for, was there hope of adoption? Was there a man back in the city, someone with a lick of yellow hair?

"The social worker's name was Deb," Pamela said to sidetrack them. "She had a Midwest accent, maybe Minnesota."

"All right, we believe you," her mother said.

"Why foster parenting exactly, is what I want to know," Denise said.

Denise and her husband Arthur had five little stairsteppers, identical blonde children that budded off Denise once a year like sea sponges. Arthur made good money in the electronics industry, enough for their Tudor Revival, for all those children, for Denise to not work and to go around in skinny pants made of shimmery black material. Her holiday pants.

"I wanted to help. The social worker was very persuasive," Pamela said.

A credible answer would have been *All of a sudden, I felt an emptiness in my life*. Denise would have seen a crevasse open up inside Pamela, a long stretch of quiet years passing. She'd have felt embarrassed at her life's riches and let it go.

Pamela didn't mention Felix.

Before the holiday there was a fight. He knew it didn't make them a real family—he kept saying this, that he understood how things were—but he wanted to spend the holiday with her and Butterbean. He wanted to see Butterbean's face on Christmas morning, those mounds of presents he'd bought for them arranged under Pamela's tree. It was cold, she knew, but if she wasn't careful Felix would insinuate himself further into her life, into the apartment. He'd already started bringing little gifts for Butterbean, dropping by to ask if she needed anything, then sticking around until all hours. He'd be living with them by Easter.

Felix's voice reached a squeaky pitch as he pleaded with her. Pamela heard herself saying she was going to her parents' for the holiday. Now here she was, confusing her family by showing up with a baby. Confusing them by showing up at all. Felix saw through her. In the six years she'd lived in the apartment above his, he never remembered her going anywhere for the holidays. This was why he'd said that thing about her, the awfulness she couldn't forgive.

You're the one regressing, Pamela. Curling up into yourself. You'll curl up so far there won't be room for anyone else. One day you'll curl up so far your atoms will fuse and there won't be anything left. You'll curl so far up they'll put up a sign that will read "Here is a person. who used to exist. Here is a person who shut out the world."

That evening, after the gifts were exchanged, Pamela and her mother took Butterbean upstairs and put him in the crib, which had been Pamela's once.

"Oh-wee-ohh-wee-oh," sang Butterbean. Kicking his legs like he did on the woman's mantel shelf, he wondered why he couldn't sit on the shelf here. It was a perfectly good shelf. It was in the room with all the presents, but the room was now an impassible ocean of ribbon and tissue paper. There was an ocean where he was before. It surrounded everything and he couldn't cross it because of the things in it. That must have been why.

"Hush singing, now, Butterbean," Pamela's mother said.

The singing stopped, and he grabbed his feet, thinking what it meant to have a grandmother, a place to spend summer holidays. To have an aunt, cousins, people with shared histories but who'd come out *different*. He kicked his legs happily at the thought of family pictures and Easter egg hunts.

When he'd settled down, Pamela's mother curled his hair lick around her finger.

"I've been trying to figure out who Butterbean reminds me of," she said. "It's that awful doll you had, the one that laughed like a demon."

"That horrible thing," Pamela said.

"I never knew why you wanted it. It was just lifelike enough to be disturbing. But it had a little skootch of yellow hair over its forehead, just like Butterbean. Wonder what happened to it?"

Local woman's windup doll circles globe, returns home decades later. Thirty years was enough time for anything to come full circle.

• • •

In her twenties, Pamela went on the pill, even though she wasn't having sex. It seemed smart and prepared, like life was a desert of shifting sands and she could be thrown onto a new track any minute. The nurse explained how things worked, hormonally.

"All those eggs you were born with, they stay right up in their basket."

It made her feel like a hen. Every time she took her pill, she said *cluck cluck cluck*.

About that same time, she started having the baby dreams. In the most common one she was unemployed, facing eviction and the threat of moving back in with her parents. Because she still wasn't having sex, she ran through the other possibilities:

>1. Immaculate conception
>2. Alien impregnation
>3. Asexual reproduction, like a sea sponge, budding off itself

She'd lie in the bathtub pretending to be a sponge, her fibrous skeleton swaying in the current.

When the baby came out, it was a litter of kittens that went running off in every direction. As hard as she tried, she couldn't hold onto even one.

• • •

One day, Pamela came home from work, and Butterbean wasn't there. Not on the mantel shelf, not anywhere.

"Butterbean, Butterbean?" she called into every room. The only response was the echo of her own voice through the apartment.

That Butterbean might disappear as suddenly and as mysteriously as he'd come had been somewhere in her thoughts all this time. Felix asked once what they'd do if that happened. Was there a missing children hotline for paranormal babies? She'd said she would call the police, of course, what any parent would do. But she didn't. She knew Butterbean wasn't kidnapped or down a well like Baby Jessica. The fold in space had opened back up, and he'd rolled into it. That was all. She sat down and listened to her empty apartment, to her life clicking along with the radiator. She curled into herself.

Local woman falls into the abyss.

A few months after Butterbean disappeared, the baby dreams started again. Pamela took a few weeks of personal leave and sat around the apartment watching *Kathie Lee & Hoda*, waiting for him to reappear. She ignored Felix's knocks at the door, his text pleads blooping into her quiet. *I'm sorry for what I said. Is Butterbean ok? The Persian place has a new vegetarian kabob.*

Eventually the knocks and texts stopped. Pamela started hearing voices through the bathroom vent that told her Felix had met someone. She took to lying on the tile and listening to his dates as they prepared food that popped and sizzled and reminded Pamela that she was alone. She eavesdropped as on a string of small conundrums were quickly worked through (Persian or Lebanese, cumin or ground marjoram) and endless arguments about which independent film directors were best. Often the theme music from *Battlestar Galactica* played in the background. She heard all the explosions when the Cylons caught up with the fleet.

"Where's your soy sauce? We can't eat this without soy sauce. It'd be, like, a travesty," whoever the woman was said one night. The woman inserted *like* into her speech pauses so often Pamela had to put a pillow over the vent. She went back to watching *Frasier* reruns on Netflix.

Local woman hits bottom.

When Butterbean didn't rematerialize, Pamela fell back into a routine at Organic Aromatics. The spacetime continuum, or whatever had ripped, had repaired itself. The gears of her life started grinding again. She wrote press release after press release, had lunch in the employee cafeteria, a corporate suited person in a sea of Oompa Loompas. The Oompa Loompas only talked about work, how you had to get the pH right or people's scalps would erupt in lesions.

Local woman considers career change.

In the spring, a reporter asked to tour the factory for an in-depth on the all-natural craze. He got high on the Epsom salts and menthol in the Crème de Mental mini-bombs, and Pamela had to cast a spell to keep it out of the paper. *Crème de Mental mini-bombs are made of carefully tested, all-natural ingredients you have in your kitchen pantry. If used as directed, they transport consumers to another world, a place of relaxation and well-being.* The reporter disappeared without a trace.

Pamela didn't go to work so much as it came to her. She began to wonder if the whole Butterbean thing had been one of her dreams after all, a past-life thing, anything other than the reality of rocking a flesh-and-blood baby while David Letterman's tooth gap filled the television screen.

Then in June, an eyelid appeared in the foot salve, its long curling lash intact. *The owner appears to have been female*, she wrote. They didn't have to worry that it belonged to one of the Oompa Loompas because all the employees on the foot salve floor were male. No one came forward to claim the eyelid.

That night, Pamela gave birth to twins in a dream. The first baby was a standard baby, nothing gelatinous. She cradled it in her arms, terrified at the prospect of motherhood but relieved she was no longer alone.

"Not so fast," the doctor said when she asked if she could take the baby home. "There's one more coming out."

At first, she thought the second baby was a flounder. She'd dreamed of birthing fish before, pasty-white slabs of grouper and tilapia slithering through the doctor's arms onto the floor, but it was in fact a giant eyelid, its long, curling lash intact.

"Someone must have mucked around with the chromosomes," the doctor said.

The nurse cocked her head and smiled, hoping to be half this lucky someday. Maybe she'd have a toenail or a couple of teeth still embedded in a hunk of gum.

Pamela hugged the babies close, wanting to be alone with them, but the others in the room closed in on her. She didn't blame them. All they wanted was to share this moment, be there when the news crew arrived. Maybe they'd be quoted on the air, something about life rolling inexorably into the next generation, in spite of everything. In spite of toes in shampoo bottles and Cylons and what you had to leave behind for moments like this to exist. But mostly, everybody wanted to see the eyelash. They all wanted a closer look at that.

We Are Still Here

1.

The Johnsons arrived at the front gate of Ghost Village like many visitors did, in a station wagon that had recently turned over to 100,000 miles.

"Come on, Flo, come on," Mr. Johnson said as he gunned the wagon's engine up the winding mountain road.

He often spoke to the car as if it were a person who understood him, and on his long commute to work each day he poured out his heart to her. Flo bore witness to each of his regrets, the risks he didn't take because he was distracted with fleeting pleasures. When he was a college student he wanted to be a disc jockey, not an insurance adjuster. He wanted to march in a political demonstration that in twenty years people would see as a historical linchpin, bridging an era of inequality with something better. Flo understood this.

Mrs. Johnson had wanted to go to Disney World. There was a hotel inside the park with a pool shaped like Mickey Mouse's head you could lay beside and sip cocktails like Raquel Flipping Welch, but she got the Daniel Boone Motor Lodge, whose pool was empty due to a fungal contamination, and the only cocktails were what she smuggled in the cooler.

"It'll be great, you'll see," her husband said, sensing her resolve to fry like a griddlecake was fading.

He won most battles this way. She imagined he used a similar strategy at work, with people whose lives had been destroyed by floods and fires.

• • •

Inside Ghost Village, with her children sprinting toward the roller coasters, her husband gone in search of a saloon rumored to serve beer, Mrs. Johnson didn't know what to do with herself. She didn't know what to do with herself a lot of places. Sometimes she would push a cart around the supermarket with no clue as to what she was there to buy. Kiwi fruit? Brie? She had a list, but suddenly it was all things no one needed, things that seemed designed to weigh a person down. When this happened she would put the cart back in its rack and drive home emptyhanded.

Mrs. Johnson had what her friends called *strange fantasies*. She had this one about leaving behind the modern world and roughing it on the prairie if there were still prairies. On the frontier there were no cocktail parties, no need to small talk with her husband's boss and his wife, who she was pretty sure were swingers. There were no supermarkets to become overwhelmed in. On the prairie, there would be peace and quiet, no Nintendos blooping in her life's background.

As if her thoughts summoned the clapboard barns and log cabins from the asphalt, Mrs. Johnson found herself wandering into Frontier Junction, the section of the park devoted to America's pioneer roots. A woman in a prairie dress was giving a milking demonstration in one of the barns, pulling at a cow's rubbery pink teats while onlookers gaped.

"Haven't these people ever seen a teat before?" Mrs. Johnson asked the woman beside her. The woman stepped away.

In the next exhibit, another woman in a prairie dress was demonstrating how to card wool, and a third was churning butter. It was all vaguely similar to the work Mrs. Johnson did at home. She thought of herself shucking corn in a calico dress and could see her life stretching out in front of her like a vast wheat field that went on and on without any trees or mountains all the way to the horizon.

What kind of fantasy was that? she wondered. Didn't most people fantasize about winning the lottery, sleeping with a celebrity? The women in her circle all had it bad for Michael Douglas, but she was sure he was exactly like any other man you could pick up on the street, probably worse. Celebrities didn't know how to do things for themselves.

Feeling undone by the pioneer exhibits, Mrs. Johnson left to watch a clogging performance in the Frontier Follies Playhouse. The troupe members were dancing their hearts out, going at it with all they had to *The Devil Went Down to Georgia*. Mrs. Johnson was a clogger in her youth and could remember dancing with that same passion, the feeling she was clogging *toward* something. She'd have gone all the way to the top if her knees hadn't given out.

Mr. Johnson was not disconcerted by the past in the way his wife was. He disappeared into the Wild, Wild West section, which had a blacksmith, a general store, and a barber shop where you could get an old-fashioned shave with a straight razor. Watching a staged gunfight from the porch of the saloon, he thought: *This was when people really got to feel alive.*

. . .

The Johnson children took in the park like it was their main oxygen source. Sated by four-dollar corndogs and deep-fried Snickers bars, they felt themselves expanding to the size of the earth as the concerns of their daily lives melt off. The need for headgear, their changing, embarrassing bodies, whoever was president after John Quincy Adams, none of this mattered on the Thunderbolt.

They'd come all the way from Florida just for the Thunderbolt's triple loop-de-loop, its zero-G drop that was supposed to make riders feel weightless. So when they saw the sign on the ticket podium saying the ride was permanently closed, twins Chad and Thad Johnson felt cheated.

"Say what?" they said in unison.

The state had just condemned the Thunderbolt due to hazardous wear and tear on the load-bearing beams. The next best thing was the Apocalypse, whose hundred-foot drops and horizontal corkscrew sounded okay, they guessed.

"Made this one kid barf yesterday," claimed the operator. "Name was Rooney."

The Johnson children waited in line amid cardboard zombies and the sounds of mines exploding, thinking how if your name was Rooney you probably had a pretty soft life. It might not have been saying much that something made you barf. After an hour-long wait, they piled into their car and jiggled the safety bar up and down, a signal that it was time to rock and roll. A recorded message barking out of the PA system warned them to turn back: the end of the world had come.

"Who's ready to get this show on the road? Let me hear you get rowdy!" the operator yelled without taking the cigarette from between his lips.

They hooted and pushed their fists into the air like Rocky, ready to have the flesh gnawed from their bones.

As the coaster taxied up the first hill, young Paul Johnson's courage failed. He'd only gone on the ride because his parents said they all had to stay together, and here he was, seconds from going over the brink, his stomach flip-flopping the way it did when he talked to girls. As he plunged down the hill, a thought appeared in his mind like a single pinpoint of light. He had a bag of cat's eye marbles in his pocket and couldn't remember cinching it closed.

"Oh, turdballs," he said, using the cuss he'd been trying out lately.

When the train reached the apex of the first loop, the marbles spilled out at the same time a rusted girder was working itself free. The process had been going on for years, the microscopic areas of rot slowly coalescing until they formed a hole. On its way into the corkscrew, the train slid off the track, and the people in the back three cars were dumped from their seats.

On the ground, Paul looked at the cracked skulls surrounded by his marbles on the pavement and assumed the marbles, his failure to cinch the bag tight enough, were the cause. Chad and Thad silently accepted blame, too, because Paul had been their responsibility.

The staff loaded the guests onto the chairlifts and the funicular railroad and sent them down to the parking lot, away from the tragedy, promising the park would be up and running the next day. This would all be just a bad memory, they said, nothing a jumbo corndog and a visit to the Shaking Shack couldn't fix, but they knew this was the end. The owners were already on the horn. They couldn't afford the lawsuits that were a sure thing once the victims' families emerged from their grief.

"Maybe Dollywood is hiring," the staff thought. They couldn't imagine Dolly Parton leaving anyone hanging, unable to make ends meet.

When they cut power later that day, everything stopped. The barrage of country music over the loudspeakers, the taffy-pulling machine, the popcorn poppers, the fry vats sizzling elephant ears and bacon-wrapped sticks of butter, the Ferris wheel, the lazy river, the funicular and chairlifts—everything froze as it was when the manager pulled the plug.

2.

The couple in the Prius zipped up the mountain in spite of the sign, which said the park was closed for renovations. The wife had gone there on summer vacations as a child and wanted to see if everything was as she remembered it.

They were on their honeymoon, no longer Will and Gina but The Millers. A few days before, they were hanging out the windows of the Prius in San Diego and waving goodbye to their wedding guests. Jobs waited for them in New York. As they reached the western edge of the mountains, Gina felt a sense of longing ,for summers spent clambering up mountainsides and panning for gems in roadside mines.

"I don't know, Babe. Looks pretty shut down to me,"

Will said.

The sign was faded and graffitied, the lacework of potholes proof no one was maintaining the road. Will feared a blowout up there with the iffy cell reception.

His new wife was still a mystery to him in some ways. She had funny habits, like wearing socks to bed and then pulling them off with her toes. After a few days, there would be a pile of socks at the bottom of the bed. *Why not take them off before getting under the covers?* he wanted to ask but didn't because they were still a little shy with each other. He didn't want to push.

The wedding came just a year after their first date, so the trip was a transitional thing; work out the kinks of living together on the road so when they got to New York they'd feel like an old married couple. Will didn't understand Gina's need to take back roads into the past when there were modern, predictable interstates to drive into their new life. If he had his druthers, he'd have been ziplining in Costa Rica right then, but he loved her and would do anything to make her happy.

When the mountain leveled off into a parking lot, the Millers pulled up to a squat brown ticket booth strung with yellow caution tape. A sign read RE-OPENING SPRING OF 1994. In case there was any doubt the place was abandoned, two junked cars sat rusting in their parking spaces.

"Oh, this makes me sad," Gina said. "I came here three summers in a row."

The last time, she caused a pileup on the bumper cars and had to be rescued by the teenage attendant. His name was Bran, probably short for Brandon. It made her think of cereal. As an outlet for her feelings, she spent the rest of the summer writing a letter that was really just a mishmash of lyrics from Amy Grant songs. *I will be walking one day, down a street far away, and see a face in the crowd and smile.* She ate nothing but Raisin Bran until September, and Bran never wrote her back.

"Let's get out of here, then," Will said. "We're supposed to be celebrating our future, not digging up ghosts." He was starting to worry this detour was evidence of something, a morbid tendency he hadn't noticed in her before.

"Come on, try taking the service road up." Gina pointed to the gravel road running between the funicular track and the trees.

Will hoped the pitiful sight of the chairlifts would make Gina want to turn around. They were still hanging down the center of the mountain like the place had only shut down for the day, not twenty years. The only signs that time had passed were the rusted chairs, most of their yellow paint eaten away by acid rain, and the underbrush rising up to meet them.

"I'm kind of getting the creeps, Geen, . . ." Will said.

She saw them before he did. Three quarters of the way up the mountain, a chair was visible in profile against the sky. Extending from its bottom edge were two horizontal sticks she recognized as legs. Gina thought she could see the square outline of a purse being clutched by flayed fingers.

"Oh, no, Will, look."

"Good grief," he said.

Six chairlifts still contained their occupants.

"That one in the middle is empty," Will said.

"Think they jumped?"

"If they did they'll be in the underbrush somewhere. Survivors would have found a way to alert the authorities."

Will put the Prius in park and shut the engine off.

"What are you doing?" Gina asked.

"We have to see who's down there. Try using your cell to call someone while I look."

She didn't care about the jumpers. They'd died quickly. Her sadness was for the ones still on the lifts, who had to sit up there until their skin fell off. She pictured herself up there, slowly decaying. Will would have come up with a plan before that happened, she was sure.

He'd have shimmied down the cable using his belt as a makeshift belay, instructed her to put her hands in her armpits to avoid hypothermia. He was handy and capable, always doing the right thing in a way she now realized was sometimes overbearing.

When she told him about the bodies, the police dispatcher asked her to repeat herself.

"Come again?" he said. "That place has been shut down for years." He was less concerned she might be telling the truth than that she was *up there messing around*. He said she was asking for trouble.

"I don't have to ask for it. It finds me, apparently," Gina said. It felt like an admission of something.

• • •

The brush under the chairs was a thicket of shrubs that made Will think of summers back home in Oregon. The Beaver State, where he reached adulthood without seeing a single beaver. One year his scout troop leaders dumped him in the woods with only a knife, a compass and the challenge of making make his way back to camp alone. Back then he feared breaking a leg, an embarrassing search party rescue involving helicopters. Thoughts of starving in the Badlands drove him back to the car before he found the bodies.

"What's wrong with your legs?" Gina asked.

"They're itching like hell. Something I touched in the brush, I guess," he said. He clawed at a patch of skin below his right knee until Gina swatted his hand away. Her way of caring for him.

The police were on their way. It was a relief to know someone was coming to take this off their hands. After giving a statement, they could drive back into town, have some lunch at the one restaurant. They'd sit quietly across from each other and try to make room for the experience relative to their feelings for each other, and after that they'd have to get on with their lives.

3.

Mrs. Johnson was the last guest onto the chairlifts. One other straggler family, the Peppercorns from Kansas, took the three chairs ahead of them. Mrs. Johnson wanted to take the funicular, but it reminded the children too much of the roller coaster.

They almost didn't make it on. Still shaking from his ordeal, Paul locked himself in the bathroom and had to be coaxed out with an elephant ear. Thad vomited. Mr.

Johnson sold them a story about how they made it off the roller coaster for a reason—to go on living their lives and make sure those who died were remembered.

"And it's a documented fact. Chairlifts are the safest mode of transport on the planet. In all my years of taking insurance claims, I have never once paid out for a chairlift accident," he said.

"What about roller coasters?" Chad asked.

"Look, I can see Flo from here," Mr. Johnson answered.

Mrs. Johnson was relieved to finally be on the way down the mountain. Most of the other guests were already hopping off their chairs at the bottom, helped by staff as eager to flee the scene as they were.

"When we get off, let's go to the International House of Pancakes!" she called to Mr. Johnson.

Pancakes would take everyone's minds off those awful few minutes when the coaster cars hung there, the frame ticking and groaning. Then the bodies, their heads opened like cans of cranberry sauce on the asphalt. She didn't ever want to think about that again.

When the chairs stopped moving, Mrs. Johnson was thinking how good the Rooty Tooty Fresh and Fruity would be after such a horror. On a normal day, they would have kept sailing toward the control tower, where the park's photographer would snap photos of them to sell as souvenirs. But nobody wanted a souvenir of today. The people at the bottom were piling into cars, already leaving behind the memory of those cracked skulls and having dangled above their own deaths. They waved and shouted, the Johnsons longing for the stale Cheetos-and-feet smell of Flo's cabin, the Peppercorns longing for the flatter-than-a-pancake terrain of Kansas, where people didn't get stuck on mountains, but they were too far up for anyone to hear them.

4.

The Millers high-tailed it to New York on interstates, no more back road detours down Memory Lane, no more grisly discoveries making silences between them in the car.

"I want to be pregnant by the end of the year," Gina said. After what she saw in the mountains, she wanted the future to start now.

Will thought this was all moving a little fast. The night they met in the bar was only a year ago, and here they were married, saying the p-word. He had always thought of marriage as an extension of dating. The idea was to lock down a good thing so no one else could get their hands on it, then Netflix and chill for life. Maybe it would last until one of them died of old age, maybe not. You could love someone and still feel that way about your relationship with them, he was sure.

If he was excited about anything, it was his new job as a programmer for the virtual reality social network, HangOut. The platform was being hailed as the new Facebook but better. Along with traditional social media functions, like status updates and photo sharing, users could host virtual birthday parties, drinks with coworkers, college reunions. With the help of the company's patented VR technology, they could experience an almost full range of personal interactions without ever leaving the house. The tagline from the marketing campaign said it all: *Be there. Without being there.* Will would be in the office connecting agoraphobes with other agoraphobes in a matter of days.

Seven hours after leaving the mountains, they pulled off the road outside D.C., checked into a Holiday Inn and walked next door to the Bob Evans, where Gina ordered the macaroni and cheese with a side of mashed potatoes.

"Didn't you have that for lunch at Cracker Barrel?" Will asked.

"Yeah, why?"

He thought of the glucose heights being reached in

her veins. All those free radicals, the stress on the adrenals.

"Just noticed, is all."

"I'm ignoring you." She held up a palm and worked the crossword puzzle printed on the tablecloth.

Will wasn't in the mood to talk anyway. The poison oak rash on his legs was blistered up and oozing some kind of yellow goo. What was he thinking, going into the brush wearing shorts?

His finger hovered over the Candy Crush icon on his phone. He wasn't in the mood for that either. He wasn't in the mood for any of this, not this Bob Evans or a dip in the hotel pool that Gina had suggested. What he really wanted was to see the skeletons again. He hadn't been able to get them out of his mind since leaving the mountains.

It probably wasn't cool that he took photos, but no one would have believed him otherwise. The shots were grainy zoom-ins, the people barely identifiable as corpses in lift chairs. The denatured souls in the front chair had their arms around each other, as he imagined he and Gina would if they were spending their last moments together.

"What's an eleven-letter word for annihilation?" Gina asked.

"Excoriation."

Will put his earbuds in and started the video of his talk with the police officer, recorded in case they were accused of something later. The first thirty seconds were his windbreaker flapping in the breeze and Gina off in the background saying *Oh my God, oh my God, oh my God.* Then he heard himself asking the officer how a thing like this goes undiscovered. Didn't the people's extended families miss them? Weren't alarms raised when they didn't show up for work? How does a thing like that even happen?

Will would remember what the officer said for the rest of his life:

They could have died up there, sure, or they could have been killed somewhere else and moved. Posed to look like tourists. There's really no limit to the sick things people will do.

Gina was still hyperventilating on the inside. The paramedic who strapped an oxygen mask to her mouth said to try and put it out of her mind. *Focus on the next step you have to take, the next problem you have to solve. Getting off this mountain, for starters.* It was probably how he could stomach a career based in tragedy. His name was Duane Pickles, and he had a tattoo on his forearm that read *Too blessed to be stressed.*

Keep on trucking, he'd said.

That's what she was trying to do, in this Bob Evans, on the rest of this trip, with the rest of her life. She'd think one step ahead of herself the whole way: D.C., Pennsylvania, New Jersey, Manhattan. She had a job lined up in public relations. It and the children would occupy her thoughts for at least the next twenty years. She would keep on trucking.

"Just not on chairlifts," she mumbled.

"What?" Will asked.

"Nothing. What's a seven-letter word for preserve?"

"Mummify."

"What are you doing?"

"Looking at pics of this guy I know's new baby."

He was logged into HangOut, waiting for the video to upload to his honeymoon album. It was loading slow, something he'd have to take a look at once he was on the job.

"Let me see," Gina said. All of a sudden babies were interesting.

Several of Will's high school classmates and former coworkers were announcing minor frustrations in the news feed, things no reasonable person would be upset about. He felt depressed reading the details of their lives. Of all the things they could have shared with the universe, they chose infected hangnails and neighbors who fired up noisy weed wackers on Sunday mornings. He thought about unfollowing them, maybe cutting them out of his life entirely. He wondered if their experiences could absorb what he was about to show them.

5.

Mrs. Johnson clutched her pocketbook, a sturdy leather Etienne Aigner made to stand the test of time even if her body wasn't. These days she was all infrastructure, all cavities and slots between bones, once brimming with her life force. Her eyeballs were one of the first soft places to go. It made sense that birds would want them while they were still soft and squishy like grapes.

Her husband was gone, too. On the second day he and Mr. Peppercorn tried to go for help, using their belts as makeshift belays to shimmy down the cable. They must not have made it because no one ever came. There were just the thumps and the yells, then quiet for decades.

When the rescue vehicles and the crime scene van raced up the mountain, the kids clapped.

"We're finally saved!" they said.

"This rescue isn't for you," Mrs. Johnson told them. She'd quit beating around the bush a long time ago.

The only people who were loaded into the ambulance were the young couple who found them. The wife was hyperventilating. The husband's legs were beginning to ooze. Mrs. Johnson could have told him the brush beneath her was full of poison oak.

"City slickers," she said.

They were a young, soft couple, the type that didn't exist in her generation. Mrs. Johnson could remember Vietnam, the missile crisis, energy shortages, the moon landings, the Voyager launches, Chappaquiddick, Iran Contra, and Son of Sam. She knew what it meant to struggle and grind, to be horrified at the world around her while good people stood by and did nothing. To exhilarate in knowing that the universe was enormous and she just a speck of stardust in it. She'd never hyperventilated that she could recall. And look at her, she was still there.

In a Dark Wood

In the lost children stories, the children make it out alive. They save themselves. There's a thing in them that's just as dark—maybe darker—than what's trying to eat them, and they find they can cook and eat someone, that it's not hard once you know how. And people taste a little like pork.

At least, this has been my experience.

When Jess shoves a corner piece of the house into her mouth, I warn her appearances can be deceiving. She says, "When do we ever get to eat off a gingerbread house?"

Also, we're starving.

"I never cared for gingerbread, myself. Too peppery," I say.

"This is not the time to be persnickety."

My stomach is growling for something salty that had a face once. Jess hands me a gingerbread man from the yard, the closest thing we have to a burger.

"Please, eat something, Esme."

I wouldn't drink the water. I wouldn't suck on the tall red grass Jess found by the pond that made her mouth look like she'd bitten someone. She claimed it took the edge off the hunger, but I said the edge would come back.

Three days since we left home. We still don't know why the Councilors came with the bombs that made everyone hit the ground, clutching their eyes. We don't know if anyone's left. When I heard the boom in the town square, I ran into the Walgreen's and got Jess. She wanted to run into the library and hide among the stacks, but they gassed it, too. We've been lucky through this.

"Eventually, the pendulum will swing back the other way. We have to be ready," Jess says. She believes the universe has an intelligence, rationing out fortune and misfortune to keep everything in balance. Our good luck streak, if you can call it that, could run out any minute.

I can't argue with that. I bite the head off the gingerbread man, and that's when I see the woman at the window, watching us. She's been there this whole time, listening.

I almost don't see her because her face nearly recedes

into the dark room behind her. She's all eye sockets and cheekbones, like she hasn't eaten in a while either, which seems unbelievable given the circumstances. I think maybe she's just lonely, that the way she's looking at us is a different kind of starvation. It's easy to see her luck is long gone.

"She lives inside food," Jess whispers, but the woman's ears are sharp from living in the woods. She comes outside, makes a corny joke about eating herself out of house and home.

. . .

The icing was laced with something, but Jess seems okay. She chats the woman up, searching her for weak spots we can use if we have to. It's how she rolls. She acts interested and people buy it so they'll tell her anything. It's gotten us out of some jams. I feel like I'm listening to Jess and the woman underwater, their speech warping and swimming away from me.

The woman's name is Beryl, a weird name for someone who wants to eat you. A lot about this isn't as it should be.

"Like, where's your oven?" I ask.

"I use the microwave. Lean Cuisines and stuff

mostly," Beryl says.

Jess gets a few nuggets out of her. Beryl was a journalist in the legislative district, back before they started rigging the elections. She quit because she felt like she was feeding the beast, helping drug the masses with information that didn't empower them.

That doesn't sound right. Witches don't have careers, concern for the working class. I'd sort it out, but my brain's a thick soup from the roofie she slipped me. After Beryl has swirled her fingers around in it, she licks them all clean.

"Tomato," she says. "Not bad."

• • •

Beryl's got a gumdrop patch out back. I don't know if it's there or a hallucination brought on by the gingerbread, but the two orange drops Jess has in her arms look real and are the size of jack-o-lanterns.

"Take as much as you want," Beryl says, licking her lips. "Stay as long as you like. My sweet girls."

I can tell Beryl's been alone for a long time. Her eyes are wide and hungry for us, like she might eat us if we try to leave. A *Misery* kind of thing where she's Kathy Bates and we're James Caan, only for now we got legs we can run out of here on. When Beryl goes in to heat us up three Lean Cuisines, I tell Jess we gotta book.

"She wants to eat us or make us wear baby clothes and call her Mama or some bullshit."

Jess's arms are gumdrop heavy. The Black Forest cricks and groans around us, and the thorny vines snake out of the trees as whatever's in the woods closes in on us. I think Beryl's connected to the forest somehow. It must be how she hears, how she knows what we're about to do.

There's a story about a witch who lives in the forest. Nobody believes in witches now, but they still don't go beyond the edge of the farmland, even to go after a lost sheep, because in the story the oven doors are wide enough for a grown man. What do you lose by playing it safe?

"I've got an Asian sesame chicken and two macaroni and cheese. First come, first serve," Beryl calls out the kitchen window.

"Macaroni!" Jess says.

"If we screamed no one would hear," I whisper as softly as I can, so the forest can't leak this to Beryl. "Even if they heard, they wouldn't come."

Jess drops the gumdrops. They roll down the hill like rogue pumpkins and disappear into the trees.

"I'm not leaving. Screw that old bag of bones," she says.

I didn't mean for Jess to hurt Beryl, not like that. We could have taken our chances in the forest, knocked her out and stole some food. We could have seen if we made it out the other side, where there had to be help waiting.

When I see the body on the kitchen floor, Jess has already removed its clothing and sliced off its fingers and toes.

"She didn't put up much of a fight," she says, like we'd cut in front of her at the supermarket.

We dig a pit out back, roast the body and move into Beryl's house. Jess carves her up like a Thanksgiving turkey. When we're done eating, she puts the fingers and toes in a sack and buries them under the gumdrop patch. Every night when the moonlight hits it, I'm sure the forest is listening to me and think I see hands coming out of the ground. Trying to claw their way back to the world of the living. After a few years I stop seeing them.

Jess makes me a Lean Cuisine and a hot chocolate, rubs my shoulders and says, "See? It was easy."

At some point, she makes a sign at the edge of the forest that reads *What you've heard is true. We cooked and ate an old woman. Her name was Beryl.* I tell her it's in poor taste, but no one's ever followed us in here.

Neil deGrasse Tyson

Neil deGrasse Tyson has a tiny solar system orbiting his head. Mercury, Venus, Earth, Mars, even Pluto, the reject, circumnavigating his person. He looks at me with those puppy-dog eyes, those deGrasse eyes that can melt you. He's the hot plasma miracle holding everything together.

"You want anything, Dr. Tyson? Nilla wafer?"

It's all I've got in the house, he can take it or leave it. I warned him when he came at me looking for love, I'm not fancy. He's seen the ratty armchair that smells like fish sticks, same as everything else in this house. He's sitting in the thing.

"Stop calling me that," Neil deGrasse Tyson says.

"OK. *Neeeil.*"

"Maggie, come on."

"You want a beer, Sugarpants?"

Neil deGrasse Tyson squirms in the ratty armchair, sinking low because its springs are shot. Any minute now, he'll fold up like a clamshell and fall right through a hole in the spacetime continuum. Wind up wherever. I worry he thinks about bolting, like maybe this wasn't worth it. The dudes over at PBS want him to do another show. *Neil deGrasse Tyson's Infinite Universe,* as if the universe could belong to a person. He really just wants to be a scientist, to spin theories, not get caught up in somebody else's thing. I want him to do it, even if it means he'll always be on the road, even if he slips away. He's what the world needs. Huggable, brilliant.

"This isn't working out, Mags. I'm gonna crash at Wayne's for a while," Neil deGrasse Tyson says. The first I've heard of any Wayne.

Saturn crashes into Jupiter. They mix to form an even bigger gas giant on his brow, a swirly Creamsicle monster. I don't like the new planet so I name it Vestal after Vestal at the fabric shop where I work. Neil deGrasse Tyson thinks I should try harder with Vestal. Like, how will writing *For a good time call Vestal* in bar bathrooms make things better? He doesn't have to put up with her crap all day.

"Don't go, Neil. This was just getting good. *So, so*

good."

"Margaret Ellen McCormick, you listen."

He is not now nor has he ever been Neil deGrasse Tyson. Neil deGrasse Tyson lives in New York City and has a wife, and for all we know he's never even been to North Carolina. I am aware of all that. He's just Ernie, manager of the trampoline park in Greensboro. We have a bobtailed cat named Nubbin, and somewhere along the line things broke between us.

I picture Neil deGrasse Tyson at the trampoline park, bouncing in his suit and tie. *Hey, watch this*, he says, bending deep, drawing power into his legs. He bounces so hard he blasts off into the sky, then the outer atmosphere all the way to the Horsehead Nebula, where he dissolves into stardust.

"If that's not good enough, if you need an astrophysicist, well, then, I don't know," Neil deGrasse Tyson says.

He swats some interstellar dust out of his eyes, as if trying to get a better look into our future. I stick my finger in Mars, pulling it out of orbit like a cherry from a pie, and I offer it to him. I pin all my hopes for us to it.

Myrtle

The ogre living under the bridge in the park, which is basically a forest with sidewalks running through it, wants me to know she means business. Before eating people, she listens to them beg for their lives, lets them tell her things about themselves, the reasons she shouldn't eat them. She eats them anyway.

"This one guy, he had a crippled dog named Peanut. It had an extra foot growing out of its front leg."

"Great," I say.

"I'm Myrtle, by the way."

She says it like we're in line at the DMV, like we've been chatting to pass the time. Later we'll Facebook each other and get cappuccinos downtown.

"Monsters don't have names," I say. She's just The Monster, the thing that runs out teeth bared if you use the bridge after dusk.

The park has other monsters than Myrtle. There's the goblin that lives in the creek, the hag who sleeps in the picnic shelter and spits at people. I tried giving the hag money once, but I learned the hard way she wants to be left alone.

"Actually, I'm an ogre," Myrtle says. "Monster is a generic term, like saying you're from North America."

Myrtle subverts all my expectations about ogres. For one thing, the floral print shift dress she's wearing looks like it came right out of the Coldwater Creek catalog.

"And I didn't think lady ogres existed, either," I say.

"Where did you think ogres came from if there weren't any lady ones?"

"The things that get left out of stories," I say, shaking my damn head.

"I'm going to eat you," she says.

• • •

I tell Myrtle she's kind of cute, for an ogre.

"What's that supposed to mean?" she says.

It's been twelve days and she hasn't eaten me yet.

"When I think of an ogre, I think of this awful hairy thing drooling all over itself, burbling gobbledygook."

Ogres of legend are always military green and smell of dead fish. No matter how hard you try, you can't make out what they're saying except the handful of words that matter. Catch. Kill. Eat. Myrtle is different. She's bluish gray and smells like a juniper bush and doesn't eat me.

"I'm done talking to you," she says, putting her palm up.

I could fold myself into Myrtle's warmth. I could smell juniper berries all day. I want to ask her if she really means to kill me, if she's just been fronting this whole time, but this seems like the fastest way to get eaten.

Frank wants to know, why give the ogre the time of day? Why give your destinies the chance to intertwine, Opal? "Opal, Opal, Opal," he says, as if I'm a child who's brought home a rabid raccoon. I talk about Myrtle every night over the vegetable lasagnas he unstacks for us out of the freezer. For months now, it's been nothing but vegetable lasagna.

"You got your mushrooms, you got your eggplant, you got your spinach, you got nutrients out the wazoo," he said once when I asked for something else. What else could I ask for? I wasn't complaining, just asking him to throw a casserole into the mix every now and then.

Frank is a practical-minded man. He chooses the most straightforward path, keeping complications to a minimum, and always knows where everything is. We're unlike in this, that I won't fold clothes when they come out of the dryer, and I'm content to live out of laundry baskets.

"Frank doesn't want you to be happy," Myrtle says.

"Frank is a good man. He doesn't want me to have to struggle. I don't want to talk about Frank."

We don't talk about Frank. On the way home from my job at Starbuck's every day, I cut through the park so I can catch Myrtle up on the haps. She's always interested and never turns down food, and after a while Frank recedes into the forest.

"So, Stacey's seeing Eric, but she's still technically with Brian? Is that what you call 'an open relationship'?" Myrtle munches a shortbread cookie, working out the subplots of my coworkers' love lives. Starbuck's is a TV show to her, like sands through the hourglass. "I don't understand human couplings."

In ogre relationships, things are pretty cut and dry. The male clubs the female over the head and says, "Let's do this thing," and she shrugs and says, "Ok, I guess." Two years later there's a baby ogre. Myrtle explained it all, the ogre gestation period being comparable to an elephant's.

When I told her about me and Frank, she asked if I was sure he wasn't an ogre.

"Frank would never club someone over the head," I said. "He's a completely non-violent person." Violence would introduce chaos into the system, making things unlivable.

"I'm just saying, it sounds pretty whatever."

It doesn't take Myrtle long to figure out I'm sleeping in the park. The playground has one of those curly slides with a fort at the top, an excellent studio apartment for someone who isn't talking about Frank. The morning she finds me curled up in the fort with my Starbuck's apron for a blanket, she lectures me about safety and making myself vulnerable to dark forces.

"There are things out here," she says.

"You mean you."

"I'm out here, yes."

"But I'm not afraid of you."

"I'm responsible for your safety while you're in the park. If Frank ever finds out..."

"We said we wouldn't talk about Frank."

"That was before you started living in the park. All contracts are void as long as you're acting like a crazy person."

"Go away, Myrtle. Go eat someone."

Myrtle

"Now you're just being a jerk."

I pull my apron over my head, but it's nothing against the force of Myrtle coming at me, relentless as rain.

. . .

"Would you be a love and bring me a flat white from Starbuck's?" Myrtle asks one day. "And a biscotti? I'm hungry enough to eat even you."

These last few weeks Myrtle's looked thin and depressed. There's been a drop in slaughters since I moved into the park, and I know it's because she's been living on squirrels. And I also know that she's done this for as long as she can. I've heard her stomach rumbling through the trees. While I'm in line at Starbuck's, she'll pull a couple of bocce players off their court and gut them, turning their entrails into kielbasa ropes. When they're found three days later, still clutching their balls, Myrtle will go underground for a few days, and I'll be alone.

No one's ever starved herself for me before. It fills me with gratitude, to think I matter that much, but it also makes me feel bad. Squirrels and biscotti are not her true nature. The doughy body and sweet underbite and her care for me do not add up to Myrtle. Myrtle is more than the sum of her parts.

"I'm not going to be your errand girl anymore, Myrtle," I say when she comes back from wherever she goes after she eats people. Later she eats the Tai Chi class, out of hunger or to get back at me, who knows.

. . .

Forts are for waiting things out. Mine is for hiding from Myrtle—the mom voice she'll use when she tells me to come down, let's talk about all this. I've just curled into a perfect ball under my apron, thinking how hard it is to be friends with ogres, when a dad and his kid climb the ladder up to the fort and bust up my pity party.

"Oh, no," the dad says.

"Who is that lady?" the kid says.

"It's a hag, son. She'll scratch our eyes out if we don't get out of here."

"I'm not a hag," I say. "I work at Starbuck's."

The words must come out *rarble rarble death* because their faces break apart the way people's faces do before they run from Myrtle.

"Climb down faster, son."

I guess Myrtle followed me here to make sure I was okay. I guess she watches me when I'm in the park, in case the other monsters mess with me. I've seen them circling like used car salesmen stalking customers and can only imagine what she tells them. *She's mine*, like she's going to sell me a Corolla. At any rate, she's right there, teeth bared at the dad and his kid, a fell roar uncoiling out of her gut.

"This park's gone to pot," the dad says as they run.

"I don't know about this," I say.

"You make a choice every day to be here. We all do," Myrtle says.

I've still got my job at Starbuck's and my Y membership (how I shower). Threads to follow back if I want. Maybe I'll set things right with Frank, make up a story about a kidnapper. *He made me hand out religious tracts,* I'll say. It will offend his sense of order, and he'll fold me back into our life.

What would I do about Myrtle, though? Leave her in the park to pick off joggers and old men with metal detectors? I wonder if I can abandon her to such a life, if ogres can be mainstreamed, enrolled in community college. I could try taking her back to the apartment, where I'd keep an eye on her for a change. We'd snuggle under a blanket and watch *Grey's Anatomy*, shaking our heads at the folly of young, sexy professionals. I'd teach her not to eat people.

"Sounds like you got it all figured out," Myrtle says when I tell her. She pats me on the head like I am an adorable small child.

. . .

Myrtle says it's time we had a talk.

Until now, she's refused to let me see her hovel. I'd beg to see it, and she'd tell me to step off.

"I want to see your bed. I want to see where you go to the john," I'd say, and she'd bare her long incisors, a warning to back off. I thought she was embarrassed by her home's poverty, the one cardboard box and rusted barrel she must have had to her name. Turns out, her digs are nicer than mine.

"Don't put this on your Snapchat," Myrtle says.

Her house is a cavern accessed through the storm drain under the bridge, with cool, damp rooms labyrinthing off each other. In the walls of the cave are notches she's filled with the skulls of her victims.

"Myrtle, this place is a hot mess," I say.

A pair of pantyhose is draped over an armchair like the skin of someone's leg. When I sit down in it, I see it *is* the skin of someone's leg sucked right off the bones.

"Take it or leave it."

Myrtle's in a mood all of a sudden.

"I was invited here," I say.

"I've spoken with Frank."

"You talked to Frank? We agreed we wouldn't talk ab—"

"He doesn't think it's prudent for you to come home. Not right now. He needs some time to think. Do you have any friends you can stay with?"

My only friend is Myrtle. I had friends. Stacey and Eric and Brian from work, but they're busy lately.

"I've got my own place," I say, gesturing up toward the playground.

"That's not a life strategy, and you know it."

I could be happy here. I think of Frank and the taut, spare life we had, the endless lasagnas unstacking, and I feel no regret.

Myrtle takes me to the kitchen, cracks a tin of Spam and shows me her pets. Not live animals, but the strung-together bones of people she's killed. She's tied a bunch together into the shape of a dog.

"Her name's Peanut. She's got an extra foot growing out of her front leg there. You be a good dog now, Peanut," Myrtle says, petting her. She puts a half moon of the pink meat on a plate for me, ringed by a Saltine cracker fan. "Hey, are you on Facebook?"

"No."

"Me either."

We have our own Facebook down here in the cave. It's called talking.

"I love how Spam is always served *en geleé*, like we're Rockefellers," I say.

Myrtle clicks her index finger in the air. *Like.*

The Lifetime original movie playing on Myrtle's television is called *A Date with a Madman*, in which a divorcee, played by Dixie Carter, answers a personal ad and the guy turns out to be a killer.

"People really shouldn't leave their houses," Myrtle says.

"You ought to know."

She says it's easy to kill. People don't take precautions, or they trip over themselves looking for the good in others. I say some people are good, and she says I'm lucky to still be alive.

We don't talk about Frank, who isn't looking for me. The next day and the day after that Myrtle pulls more Spam out of storage and I make the joke about the Rockefellers every time. She laughs of out politeness because politeness is an easy gift, like not sucking the bones out of my skin.

Lark

1.

The canyon was really a mountain turned upside down.

The people who dug it were looking for gold, but they settled for copper. The scientist brought out to gauge its worth said it could conduct electricity, which was worth more than gold, so they dug. A railroad spiraled into the pit, then houses sprang up along the walls, a village in a void.

When the mountain had retracted into itself, it left a hole a mile deep and two wide. The descendants of the people who started the mine looked into the hole and thought that it was probably a mistake to order your life around a giant hole. There were other futures waiting for them, and right then they were being sucked into the hole, so the owners sold it to an international conglomerate. If you can sell a hole—if you can buy something that isn't there.

"Let someone else get up early, handle the labor strikes, the accidents that left the workers shells of themselves," they said.. They hadn't loved the business and wouldn't miss it.

The thing they would miss least of all was the train used to cart bodies out of the pit. The miners called it the Death Train. It only came when a man had been sliced in two, electrocuted, blown half to bits, his guts coiling out of his torso like Christmas garland. If you heard the train's dismal toot, it was coming for someone you knew.

"We don't want to see any of that," said the owners, who hadn't asked for this life. They held out their hands to show that they were tied.

Sometimes they stood at the edge of the canyon and looked into its mouth, at what it had become. With the mine running twenty hours a day, it was like a city at night, alive with ants operating the diggers, the haul trucks, all under the weird green glow of the work lights. It reminded the owners of the time they went to Los

Angeles and looked down at the city from a patio way up in the hills. This was like that and something else entirely. Crushed dreams, ceaseless struggle below them. At dusk the lights of the workers' shacks flicked on, the smelting plant chugged, the trains carried the ore out and returned with empty bellies. At the center of the pit, another pit. A black pit. There was probably another pit inside that.

An urban legend said the pit held the souls of workers who died on the job. One day all the angry spirits would rise up out of the hole and drag the owners down with them. Another said it contained a monster, but the owners didn't believe any of this. It was just blue-collar superstition.

Still, they wondered what kind of monster might live at the heart of a copper mine. Was it indigenous or had it been created by the things that happened in the pit? Was it the cause of the landslide fifty years before that buried half the workforce? The rumbles that shut down production, eating into profits? Who could say? And, if they were honest with themselves, who cared? Their money was in microchips now. It was such a clean way to make a living, and there were no death trains involved. Why hadn't they sold the place off years ago?

2.

I am the only soul still calling Lark home. I must be a thousand by now.

Before I got this old I ran the Victoria, the Violet Jewel of the county, faded to lavender now. And what a hotel it was, full to capacity most nights, a piano bar in the front parlor. I saw to it the boys who worked the copper mine had a place to blow off steam. When they closed the mine, the town and the bookings stopped and the piano player took his tip jar and run off, and I didn't have nowhere to go. I had no family in the next town or the next state nor nowhere, just the Victoria, which I paid for in cash earned by knifing a prospector. As it folded, the town gave no thought to me or the Victoria, which had been its heart.

Now I make do on expired cans from the supermarket. ;How the mighty have fallen. I go once a week like a real shopping trip, picking through broken glass and the vines that have snaked in from outside, the earth reclaiming this trapezoid of land, to extract cans of green beans, creamed corn, and the like. My church is a bust-up A&P. My family are the little turds from the city, tossing rocks into my windows to try and raise me.

Ruby, Ruby, come out and show us your boobies.

Without them, I'd be any old rotting woman on any old rotting porch in the rocker Theodore Roosevelt once sat in, food for maggots. I shrug into my field coat, left by a long-gone guest who never paid his bill, the cold driving down from the blue-white mountain range in front of me. The geologist who stayed here once said the mountains took millions of years to bunch up like that. A slow violence, like my skin shrinking around my bones.

3.

The hills are littered with ghost towns, as they are littered with mines. When the mines close, the towns close, and dead towns create ghosts.

Tourists like to stop here. The ones driving to Disneyland always pull over with their fanny packs and their white athletic socks stretching up to their knees and say, "Look, kids, this here is a ghost town," like there's a lesson here about failure or people abandoning their lives for something easier. The older children will peer into our windows looking for ghosts, while the younger ones scurry back to the car.

The fathers want to teach the kids about their

history. "Once this place was alive with the hum of industry. The country was expanding toward a new frontier!" The kids just want to chase ghosts. Back home they watch a program in which teams of investigators go into abandoned mental hospitals and prisons, hoping to catch spirit voices on tape. The kids are thinking of this as they break into the houses, plundering the attics for the things we left behind:: dress forms and hobby horses, an old Victrola, Barbie Dreamhouses, plastic houseplants, and other things not needed to start a new life. Everyone leaves here disappointed.

Once some kids found our playground and couldn't believe its lack. The field that was cleared for the equipment has reclaimed the space, and instead of a neat circle of shale there's grass enveloping the seesaw and jungle gym. The rusted slide ladder stands off by itself, missing its slide. We worry the kids will climb it and slide off into a black hole.

"This is the saddest playground I've ever seen," one of them said.

"I like it. It's gothic," said another one, whose black clothing suggested he was interested in death.

They got on the rusted merry-go-round, which groaned and scraped from disuse. No one had ridden it since the day the town closed. That day, before they piled into station wagons and left for towns with job markets for their parents, the kids had all jumped on for one last whirl, feeling sorry for themselves. The new houses and schools that were waiting for them had a funny foreign smell, worse than the sulfur that still lingers here. They went around a few times and then hopped off because the merry-go-round was no longer theirs and there's no joy in borrowed things.

Teenagers from neighboring counties like to break into our school. Ditching class to study our peeling paint and electrical wiring sprouting from holes in the walls, they wait until the sun goes down, then dare each other to go inside. One with a faint heart will always want to prove he's not a coward, and when he gets lost in the crumbling halls, it's we who have to lead him out.

The girls head for the washrooms. "Bloody Mary, Bloody Mary," they say in front of the mirror, spinning around thirteen times even though none of us has ever appeared in the mirror. They'll say different, that we looked back at them from black eye sockets as blood poured from our mouths and told them their doom. *You will die an untimely death at the hands of a married lover.* They have misunderstood the history of this place. They're looking for a different kind of ghost than we are.

United Parcel Service

You aren't expecting the package, which looks heavy enough to contain a bomb or a brick of something. One of your *CSI* nightmares come to life.

"Maybe you ordered something off Amazon and forgot? Maybe someone's sent you a gift?" says the United Parcel Service driver, holding the box under his arm. Without asking, he steps into the foyer and sets the box on your Biedermeier hutch.

"Just need your John Hancock on this, and I'll be out of your hair," he says.

You've got death scenarios lined up for this. You're stabbed, excoriated, defenestrated. Twelve percent of murders are committed by strangers, according to that episode of *Dateline.* A woman selling a mattress through the classifieds was dismembered oneand frozen in Ziploc bags. For weeks, the police mistook her for salmon steaks. You write *Under Duress* on the tablet in case someone is tracking this.

No one's tracking this. A wire isn't tripped at UPS headquarters, signaling entry into a client's home. Quality Control, or whoever handles breaches in protocol, is at a teambuilding retreat when he lays the tablet on the box. They're busy performing trust falls when he walks into your living room.

"Long day," he says. He collapses on the davenport and undoes the top button of his work shirt, exposing a wild triangle of chest hair. "Lady on Peach was returning some pants, and it was my fault they didn't fit, apparently. Now, let's hear about *your* day." He pats the cushion beside him.

UPS drivers don't make themselves comfortable on people's davenports. People don't hear about it on the ten o'clock news report and discuss it in checkout lines (*it was the damndest thing, how he took off his shoes and poured himself a gimlet*), yet on your davenport is a man in a brown shirt and shorts, singing a line from *La Bohème*.

"O suoave fanciulla..."

"Is there something else you need? A signature on

an insurance form, maybe?" you ask. If he's thinking of torturing you, it's best to speak in pleasant tones.

"Can't think of anything," the driver says.

When the police arrive, he's sipping his gimlet and watching *Matlock*. The episode has Don Knotts in it, and there's been a mix-up that Matlock will have to unravel.

"Ben Matlock, you sly devil," he says. He shakes his head at how easily Matlock gets the real killers, the grifters, the kidnappers, all to hang themselves. "I should have gone to law school. If I had, well, hindsight's twenty-twenty, am I right or am I right?"

The officer asks what the trouble seems to be. The driver looks up, annoyed that his program has been interrupted.

"We're having a disagreement about remodeling the kitchen, is what seems to be the trouble," he says. He takes a gulp of his gimlet as if to steady himself. "Marble countertops don't come cheap, I can tell you."

"That doesn't sound too serious," the officer says, his eyes searching your skin for signs of a fracas, his disapproval a fourth person in the room.

"But," you say.

"Sorry to have wasted your time, officer," the driver says.

As the police car backs out of the driveway, you think

of the singles cruise you have coming up. You've paid for a month on the Aegean Sea, nothing but teal water fanning out like a skirt as far as the eye can see, everything your life contains disappearing beyond its edges. When you made the reservation, you sent positive energy into the universe in hopes of meeting a nice man. Someone tidy and liberal who wouldn't put sweaty feet on your davenport. The person you had in mind was like Robert Downey, Jr. without the drug-laced past. Employed in the sciences, he is cerebral only to the point of being interesting, not making other people feel foolish. The set of fraternal twins you'd adopt together would be renamed Walter and Geraldine. You'll have to have a little talk with the universe.

. . .

You fantasize about a lot of awful things. In your scenarios you become the middle of the human centipede, an identity theft victim, the hostage in a bank robbery. Your car rolls into a lake while you're trapped inside. Your tether snaps during a spacewalk at the International Space Station, sending you drifting into the cold vacuum of space. Sometimes on conference calls at work, you lose yourself in these catastrophes and have to be called back to reality.

"Sharon? Did we lose you? Where'd we land on the Winterson account?" says the Vice President of Development.

It happens on dates, too, the few you have a year.

"Sharon? Where'd we land on that second bottle of Zin?" say the brothers and college roommates of coworkers.

In each scenario, you plan an escape route. Convince the robber you're on his side, keep a hammer in the glove compartment. Pass on the second bottle of Zin. The only scenario you don't plan for is a delivery person delivering himself, making you sign for him. Putting sweaty feet all over your davenport.

. . .

Your house is a fortress the driver picks his way into each night. He tries his key and finds you've had the locks changed again. You've installed an alarm system, requiring him to cut power to the house. When he finally gets inside, he pours a gimlet and flops on the davenport, where he lets out a satisfied sigh. "The people rest, your honor." Something he lifted from *Matlock*.

You try putting the house on the market. A nice

thirtysomething couple called Knickerbocker comes to see it, their hope for the future beading on their skin like sweat. They're looking for a place with "good energy." You worry they'll see the driver sprawled on the davenport in the bottom half of his uniform and assume he comes with the house.

When the real estate agent brings the Knickerbockers inside, the driver tells them there's been some kind of mix-up.

"We love this house. We'd never sell it," he says.

The Knickerbockers fold themselves back into the agent's Miata and buy the Tudor revival on the corner.

Eventually, you accept that you live together. At 5:20 each afternoon, the brown truck rolls into the yard, and he removes his shoes and socks. Gimlet, davenport, *Matlock*. During the first year you think about purchasing a gun to scare him off but decide against it. If things turned ugly, you'd go up for Murder One.

"There isn't much you can do now. He's got squatter's rights," your lawyer says, after the driver has been in your house five years. There will be other lawyers, and they'll all say the same thing.

• • •

On your thirtieth anniversary, the driver gives you a pearl necklace. Not to garrote you with, it turns out, but a gift of love. You're only common law, but to him this is as real as if you had a church wedding with tulle rice bundles and a woman named Beverly warbling *The Lord's Prayer*.

The driver is old and tired from carrying around an enlarged prostate. On the left side of his body, ulcerous tumors eat into his arm and face. The doctor has scraped them off, but all those years driving in the sun have destroyed the skin at its deepest layers. The tumors always come back whatever he does to get rid of them.

His muscles hang flaccid from his bones. You could tear him like tissue paper. Just yesterday he slipped a disc trying to move the davenport. To get the job done, you had to enlist the Knickerbocker man. Now you think you could have moved the davenport yourself. You feel strong enough to throw the Biedermeier hutch.

You throw the pearls instead. Into the fire, built by the driver's own hoping-for-romance hands. Why did he think he'd get some? In all these years, you've never let him touch you.

The pearls blacken in the fire, holding together until the string burns away and the tiny black globes bounce off the hearth. You once read that breaking a string of pearls was a bad omen, a sign everything is about to fall apart.

You don't know what it means to burn one, if that makes things worse, and if it does, for who?

"Sharon, that's a genuine Mikimoto! Have you lost your marbles?" the driver says.

He picks up the hot black pearls and cleans the soot off them with spit, protecting them in his cupped palm. Pearls don't burn, was the other thing you read. It's how you know they're genuine.

"It's nice, but I'd rather you moved out," you say.

The driver looks up, a thumb-shaped smudge of soot under his lip. His mouth hangs open, weighted down by jowls. "I'm eighty years old. Where would I go?"

"The old folks' home? The YMCA? A halfway house?"

When he tries to get back on the davenport, you kick him in the shin.

"You're cracked, Sharon. *Non compos mentis.* What's gotten into you?" he says, rubbing the kick mark on his lower leg.

"Stay off my davenport." You kick the other shin.

The driver ends up on the floor, cradling his shins. A line appears on the carpet in front of you, with everything that's already happened in your life on one side and everything that's yet to be on the other. You know your next move will define you as a person, one who allows herself to be carried by the current of time or who pilots her own existence. Taking the road less traveled, like in the poem.

You want to kick the driver's scrotum, but there isn't time for that. You open the door and roll him outside in the carpet. When he's climbed back up the hill and sees you've barred the door with the davenport, he gets into the UPS truck, by now an old junker. The engine turns over after the fifth or sixth crank, and then he's gone.

. . .

When word gets around you've kicked the driver out, the picketers come.

"The old folks' home was full, you jerk," they say. He's been living in the truck next to the Wal-Mart, and they've set up a crowdfunding campaign to get him back on his feet.

"You're a monster," they shout.

"He let himself in. I couldn't get him to leave," you insist.

"You're full of it."

They demand to see the bruises, the shiners, the locksmith receipts. How can they take your word for anything they can't see with their own eyes? You try turning the question on them—how can you trust they're who they say they are, not monsters themselves—but they turn it back around, how you don't get to ask them things, how you don't have the right.

"Come out, lady," they shout. "These signs took us hours to make."

What a disappointment you must be, sealing yourself up inside the house, your experience taping curtains around windows finally good for something. The picketers give up and start circling a vacant lot. When the lot is filled with modular housing, they move to the quarry, which they claim is a safety hazard. No one has fallen in since that one kid ten years back who rolled down the side like a big log and into a pile of department store mannequins. If you're remembering the story correctly, he climbed out on his own, more embarrassed than hurt.

"That doesn't make it okay to leave a giant hole in the earth," the picketers insist. "One tragic accident would be one too many."

The hole is filled in with earth and turned into a skating rink, and so on and so on, until the world is exactly how they want it.

• • •

One day you're sweeping the foyer and notice the package

still sitting on the hutch, a coating of dust on the outside and the corners mouse-chewed. You're expecting a cloud of anthrax or a poison dart flicked from a miniature catapult but find only a bathing suit with a parrot embroidered on the front, a floppy coral sunhat and espadrilles.

"The trip!"

The singles cruise, how could you have forgotten? It was to Greece, you think. No, Cyprus. Or was it Italy? Something about teal water fanning out around you. A water skirt. You planned to tell people you met on the boat your name was Vivian. Women named Vivian were always sure of themselves, grabbing life by the balls, so to speak, and you liked the idea of pretending to be someone like that. You thought if enough people called you Vivian, that's who you'd eventually become.

You slip out of your housecoat and into the bathing suit. It doesn't fit, but that's not the point.

. . .

You've been a shut-in so long many of the neighbors don't know who you are. If they do, they know only of a scandal years back, a black widow who hid inside until she became a brown recluse. You aren't sure what stories have sprouted from you and walked away on vines, how near or far from the truth they've flowered, but they aren't good stories, you know that.

"Ma'am, do you need help? Do you need something?" the neighbors ask as you walk toward the highway in the parrot bathing suit and the espadrilles and the floppy hat.

"Not a thing," you say. You walk in the direction you think blue water might be.

When you've left the town behind, you're in a wilderness in which you're not afraid because bear attacks are at a century low. Sex slavers are unlikely to be interested in you.

"Who'd abduct an old woman?" you ask the trees, who don't answer. They've got their own problems. They're disappearing row by row, recycled into condominiums with ocean views.

You wonder what far-off place you're pointed toward. The Black Sea, perhaps? You've always wanted to see if for yourself, to find out if the water is really black or that's just what people call it. In your mind, it's a glittering purple-black ocean filled with scorched pearls.

You press on into the forest. Every now and then a hiker or government surveyor comes along and asks if you're all right. Have you wandered off from your caregivers? Lost your dementia pills in the woods? Can they give you a ride to the old folks' home?

"No, not there," you say, putting as much space between you and them as you can. "The driver might be living there."

After the quarry, the picketers had picketed the old folks' home and shamed the owners into building an addition. You worry the driver would move into your room and everything would start all over again.

You keep walking until the woods peter into an apricot beach rimming an ocean. You blink in the bright sunlight, as all those years as a shut-in having accustomed you to dimness. The water shifts from blue to ultramarine to bright moss green at its edges, and on the opposite shore sprout the cobalt blue domes of houses. There are people at the water's edge waving you to them, chanting something that sounds like *Vi-vi-an, Vi-vi-an, Vi-vi-an*.

It's easy as pie, sliding into the warm water. Looking back, you see the apricot beach expanding, engulfing the forest and the town with the old folks' home, the driver and your davenport and the Knickerbockers, until everything your life once contained is buried. The sand takes the picketers and the old quarry, the house you grew up in on Plum Street with the red gingham curtains in the kitchen window, the nieces and nephews in distant cities. It blankets the high school where you once played a solo on the French horn, and the office building you worked in until you retired, with its labyrinth of gray cubicles folding back on itself. All these pieces of your life sink beneath the sand, slipping out of your head as you circle your arms in the deepening water and push toward the other shore.

Theta Orionis

Colette Fossey brings a Niçoise salad, and her husband Franklin Delano brings the hot dogs. Scads of hot dogs, arranged in pyramid shaped piles on a folding table.

"I still don't understand why you needed to bring so many wieners," she says, and he laughs at her because she's said *wiener*. After he's fired up the grill, he says, "Who's ready for a dog? Get them while they're hot."

Mo and Jean bring the beer.

"It'll feel like you've been hit by a Mack truck," Mo says about the shockwave. When two bodies collide, all kinds of things happen, force-wise, gravity-wise. "Just being in the neighborhood, you feel it. Nothing in this part of space happens in a vacuum." He laughs at his own joke, lame even for an astrophysicist.

Clarissa and Arthur bring potato salad. Early in their marriage, Clarissa had an affair—not a love affair, no one worth losing Arthur over or anything like that, just a terrible mistake she regretted, and nothing was ever right afterwards. They came here to repair the damage. No one eats the potato salad because they've made deals with themselves not to accept lackluster handouts from life, not to settle for the potato salads of existence. After two neighboring protoplanets have rammed into each other, after that damage has occurred, the wreckage of both bodies tearing across the sky in hot white streaks, Clarissa takes the potato salad home and eats the whole Tupperware bowl of it over the kitchen sink.

No one has to eat potato salad over the sink here, which is why Clarissa does it in secret. They know what's swirling around them. When they squirted out the other end of the G-port, they were bang in the middle of the Orion Nebula, where six rebel stars spun like dervishes around them, none of them even a half-million years old. It's a matter of local pride that their star is the most luminous in the whole nebula, lighting it up so bright you can see it from Earth. The evacuees, as they think of themselves, can remember staring up at the sky as the people they once were and seeing the nebula as a pinpoint of light below ruddy Betelgeuse, the second notch in Orion's sword.

This part of the nebula is known as the Trapezium Cluster. It was first seen by human eyes through the lens of Galileo, and now humans are living in it. It's a tight cluster of hot baby stars living fast and dying young. The evacuees are here at the beginning of things, in a place too new for mistakes to have been made. That's why they chose it. Most of them call this place The Trapezium, or The Trap for short. A handful have been here long enough to call it Home. The old-schoolers like Moe call this part of space by its older name, *Theta Orionis*.

The collision they're about to witness has taken millions of years to complete, as all collisions do. The process was set into motion when the first pieces of dust clumped together, filling the void of space with the remains of stars that blew their guts apart long ago. The dust clouds swirled and heated up, eventually collapsing under their own weight to form stars. The remaining detritus in the neighborhood continued to clump and swirl, forming baby planets like this one. There aren't rules here, not in the sense of fixed orbits, which is why Constance and Prudence are about to tear each other apart.

Sucked in by the larger proplyd's gravity, the smaller one presses into its atmosphere until the force sets both ablaze. There's a white flash of light over the mountains, then a sound like gunfire cracking, the delayed resonance of two bodies obliterating each other. As Mo predicted, the shockwave takes a few minutes to reach the group, and then they're knocked flat. People brace for it, but it's not the kind of thing you can brace for.

The collision knocks everything out of them—breath, a little bit of urine, the momentary ability to recall who they are and what they're doing here. They lie on their backs for a few moments, feeling a new solar system ordering itself around them.

The people's minds are blank tablets. *Tabulae rasae.* The woman who brought the Niçoise salad has fallen out of her chaise lounge and lies on the ground next to the man who cooked the hot dogs, hundreds of hot dogs, more than they could collectively have consumed, trying to remember the names of people back on Earth. They slip through her fingers like fine sand. It's a relief not to remember, which means life must have been awful. She might have had alcoholic parents or no parents. For all she knows, she grew up in an orphanage for children of wayward mothers. If she's strayed from the path, if the nuns failed, she's innocent of that now. She's a new planet coming to life, no experiences warping her evolution yet.

The man who cooked the hot dogs looks back at her

with eyes empty of the suffering of the past three years, empty of her, as little white pinpricks of memories begin to surface in his brain—his locker combination in junior high school (39-15-25), the name of a woman he took to the prom (Lynnette), but the woman who brought the Niçoise salad is yet a mystery to him. Everyone props the backs of their lounges back up, frowning as the past returns to them. That time the house burned down, the appendectomy, the endless conference calls about fundraising. They hold their hands to their foreheads, a bigger wallop than they expected. Clarissa suffers from migraines, so there's the worry one will come on.

"I reminded you this was a possibility," Arthur says. They have not yet, even in this place, managed happiness.

After people have recovered from the wave, they fold up their lawn chairs and break down the food tables. The woman who brought the Niçoise salad turns her eyes back to the slow-motion collision still happening in front of them. Most of the smaller protoplanet is gone, spun off into space or absorbed into the other. Molten threads arc off its shell like lava jets off a volcano. Soon the threads will reach the surface, becoming meteorites. It won't be safe outdoors for days.

The woman with the Niçoise salad knows without knowing why that this is how life starts. She knows that full planets, continents, oceans can follow from violence like this. She won't be alive to see any of it, but it's coming. The hot-dog man watches her watching until she turns and looks at him and covers his hand with hers. Tears coming over the brink.

G-ports are slits in the fabric of space. And it turns out, the universe is full of them. All you have to do is find one, fire a proton burst at its coordinates and slip inside. As the woman who brought the Niçoise salad neared the G-port that brought her here, she pictured herself zipping up in a giant sleeping bag, like on the camping trips she took with the hot dog man before the accident, and waiting out the horrors of life together.

She's still trying to place the man. She knows he belongs to her, but the details escape her, like trying to remember the specifics of a dream. To bring him into relief, she says, "Tell me something about you. Something I wouldn't care to believe."

He tells her that when he was in college he went on a date and decided halfway through the movie he didn't like the girl.

"I got up and told her I was going to the bathroom, but really I just went home."

"That's awful."

He can't argue with that. Dating was a sticky business.

In his youth, he was unable to tolerate the gritty parts of people, their unwashed bits. The girl smelled faintly of cedar and underarm sweat, like she'd dug an old hand-knitted sweater out of a chest especially for the date. He didn't want to be with anyone who would dig things out of chests for him. It seemed desperate. Hopeful in the worst possible way.

"I can't believe you never told me about that," the woman says, as though he'd omitted some vital truth of himself she won't be able to live with.

He doesn't know if he's told her this story before. He thinks her name here is Collette and she once taught science and when they came here together they had different names.

"I was nineteen," he says.

The woman thinks about the woman the hot-dog man left in the movie theater, what track her life took after he walked out. She thinks about the tour bus full of senior citizens, people's grandparents, rattling like seeds in a gourd as the bus rolled over after she collided with it. Before the accident, she'd left her travel mug of coffee on the kitchen counter. Starting the car, she decided it wasn't worth going back for.

The woman wonders: would the old people who died still be alive if she'd gone back for the mug, or would the universe have found a way to kill them anyhow? A traffic hang-up that slowed the van's trajectory out of the senior center's parking lot, a stop to let a train pass. She must have wondered this before. The man watches as this and other facts of their life return to the woman and covers her hand with his free hand, waiting for her to remember his name.

Quantum Tentacles

The waitress at the Cracker Barrel keeps calling everybody baby, like we're all in some kind of relationship. The embroidery on the front of her apron reads Jolene. This is funny because she seems to enjoy being a waitress in the same way Dolly Parton enjoys being a country music singer. I say this to Temple and the guys, meaning it in a good way, but Temple takes it wrong.

"I bet she's got a little pad at home where she writes down what her husband wants for dinner. 'You want the cornbread or the biscuits, baby?'" Temple says in this put-on Tennessee accent, or what she thinks is one.

Ray and Lionel laugh with her. There is unspoken agreement that she should do comedy.

I don't much like Temple, and she knows that. The whole trip has been her needling me, seeing how far she can push it. Yesterday she made us drive an extra half hour because she wanted a hotel with a pool and then didn't swim in the pool. I have this fantasy where I tiptoe over to her and Lionel's bed and quietly smother her with the neck pillow she naps on in the van. I could do it. They're heavy sleepers.

"Why don't you get off your high horse, Edie?" She wrinkles up her nose, trying to be cute, because when it comes to fighting with me, she knows where the line is.

Ray and Lionel are in a band, which is why we're in Nashville. It's called Quantum Tentacles, after this old horror movie I saw a couple of years ago. Classic fifties disaster plot: a sick and depraved humanity is dumping its toxic waste in the ocean, causing sea life to change at the subatomic level. There are sharks and lampreys that can make themselves invisible, fish swimming in and out of the spacetime continuum, changing the history of the planet. Just when people think it can't get any worse, a bunch of giant octopuses come squelching out of the ocean to ransack the beach towns. They're looking for who's responsible: turns out it's everybody.

The octo-freaks move fast for things with no bones. They flurp across the sand on slime and leg coils turning like tank wheels until they find someone to tentacle, trailing sticky black ink behind them. Half the movie is close-ups of suckers on people's faces.

"They have quantum tentacles," I told Ray.

"Octopuses don't have tentacles. Strictly speaking, they have arms," he said. "It's a good name for a band, though." So I guess you could say that everything that happened after that was because of me.

Back then, Ray and I were going through a rough patch, during which time I was also having a lot of nightmares about global calamity. Giant cephalopods, nuclear holocaust, the whole deal. In most of them, I ended up on my own because everyone else was dead or had left to save their own skins. In the one with the zombies, Ray left with a survivalist named Margery to get weapons. He never came back.

Temple and the guys are concentrating on their cornbread, which is filling and good in a glutinous, market-tested sort of way and makes everybody quiet down. The guys shove the yellow discs into their mouths whole, as if this is their first shot at food in weeks. Temple takes all day, tearing hers into little pieces, putting them in her mouth one by one. This is how she eats, like a raccoon.

I want us to have a nice dinner, in spite of Temple and how she is, in spite of everything. I want to show I understand the gig later tonight could change everything.

"Have you guys given any more thought to holding auditions?" I ask.

Ever since that indie paper in Atlanta wrote them up, the Tentacles have had a hipster following around the Southeast. Hornrim P. Bedhead called them the future of the Nintendocore movement, with their unexpected shades of bluegrass and gypsy punk. Ray tells people they're Depreciation Guild meets DeVotchKa meets Flatt and Scruggs, which I think assumes a lot about people's musical knowledge. On stage, he'll toodle these Super Mario Brothers synth beats while Lionel busts out on accordions, dulcimers, once a bunch of wooden spoons. The crowd eats it up.

"You just don't get it, do you, Edie?" Temple says. "What they're trying to do onstage? They're trying to create something." Her voice goes up at the ends of her sentences, telling me things I should already know. She still has some cornbread in her mouth, and it makes her words come out pasty.

"Easy, T," Ray says. "It's a valid question. Every band gets to the point where they have to evolve. I'm just not sure we're there yet." Lionel shoves more cornbread in his mouth, which is the kind of thing he does when I talk.

Temple cocks her head to the side, her lips pooched

out. Her eyebrows go up and down once. *Told you*. Back in high school, she used to do that after she'd kicked the crap out of some girl. She'd have this look of satisfaction, and usually a few hair strands caught in her fingernails. If you go back there, you can still see flecks of Megan Blackwelder's nose blood the janitor didn't get off the gym wall.

"What are you smirking at?" I ask.

"How negative a person you've become," she says. The guys sweep themselves into their own discussion, something about amps or ants or aunts, so they don't hear any of this. She says, more with her eyes than anything else, "And how big your butt looks in those jeans."

I want to knock her head off her neck, but I don't.

. . .

Cracker Barrel food is always good. In a world that could quit on you any second, it's nice to know you can pull off the interstate anywhere in America and it will be exactly like the last one you stopped at. You enter through the gift shop, with its comforting displays of angel figurines, windchimes, tubs of licorice whips and head-sized lollipops, sacks of gourmet grits, wall plaques with *Live, Laugh, Love* written on them in loopy, feel-good script.

You sit down among old tractor parts and think about simpler times. You play that little pegboard game while you wait, and then the waitress brings you food that makes you want to go to sleep.

The section we're in has a rusted wagon wheel and tin ads for motor oil on the wall. Temple is sitting under a moonshine jug that looks like it's about to come down on her head. I stare at it hard in hopes I can make it move.

She didn't want to eat here, which partly explains how she's being. She saw a sign for a truck stop on the interstate that said *Eat Here, Get Gas* and wanted to pull over, saying it would make a good story when people asked about the trip. I pointed out that it would just be a bunch of fat truckers eating those chemical pink hot dogs, and she said she feels sorry for me sometimes.

I slide the pegboard game in front of me, not especially wanting to play but knowing it irritates Temple. She says I take forever, even when the moves are obvious.

"You give me that, Edie," she says, reaching for the board. "It's like fingernails on a chalkboard watching you do that."

"It's not a race," I say, pulling it closer. What I mean is *Get out of my life*.

That fringe of flesh tubules on her neck, what she uses to breathe with, I guess, flutters like an electric current has been shot through it, so I figure she gets me.

Dolly has a tray as big as a spaceship balanced over her shoulder, sort of excessive for just four teas. I guess trays are easier to carry that way. I guess waitressing is hard on the joints, on the soul, and you have to find ways to lighten the load. If Dolly heard Temple's hick impression from before, there could well be a foamy spitwad floating in her drink. I order positive thoughts around this possibility, hoping to bring it into the world, and feel like I'm partners with Dolly somehow.

Something's happened since the cornbread that's caused her to wilt. I know because she gives everybody the wrong drink and doesn't call us baby. She looks out at the parking lot while she waits for our orders, I guess at our van with that big green octopus on the side, its tentacles curling off the edges. It's hard to miss.

"What'll you have?" she asks when it's my turn. I haven't been able to decide because there's a joke rising from my gut, one she hears twice a day at least, and she can see it bubbling up. *Jolene, Jolene, Jolene, Jolene, I'm beggin' of you, please bring me a chicken fried steak.* She's pretty much daring me to try it. Her pen hangs over the pad, its time and hers wasted.

"Meatloaf," I say.

If she had a neck fringe, it would be going crazy right

about now.

• • •

Another waitress brings our food. Janice, according to her apron. She's not here for the career advancement, this is obvious, and she slides our plates across the table hard, like she finds them offensive.

"I think you've got the wrong table," I say.

Janice looks at the ticket and then my food and then me. "Meatloaf?"

I nod. "What happened to Dolly?" I ask.

She hands me a bottle of peppers in vinegar, like that was the trouble.

I stumble up from the table and into the bathroom, pouring myself a cup of ambition to wash my hands. The waitress change at the last minute is too much to adjust to. I don't like things like that, especially here. There should be continuity, a sense that you can close your eyes for a minute and when you open them again everything's exactly how you left it, that the ground is not constantly shifting under you. I start to worry that something bad has happened to Dolly. A zombie attack in the breakroom. Some kind of ransom situation. I don't worry long because when I push into the cold bathroom there she is, bending over the sink. She looks up, and her face is like people's faces in the octopus movie: tentacled, nowhere left to run.

"Are you all right?" I ask.

"I'm doing fine, baby," she says, smiling a big white Grand Ole Opry smile. "Anything else we can do for y'all?"

"You can tell me what Janice's problem is. You can tell me why you were just crying into that sink."

She wipes her face with a paper towel, throwing it in the trash like a severed head. "I don't guess that's your beeswax."

I want it to be my beeswax. I want to slide down the wall next to each other and trace our bad decisions backwards through our lives. I have this one where I follow a trail of sticky ink into the bathroom, where I find panties that aren't mine in the hamper. Skanky thong ones, made to show over the top of someone's jeans. I want to find out if she's got one, too. I want to tell her about moving in with that bartender instead of taking the LSAT and about Temple and her tentacles and the baby they think I don't know about. It's probably got tentacles of its own, pink nubby ones just starting to bud off. When it slithers out, it's going to come for me and I'll have to run. I want to put my head on Dolly's shoulder, but something tells me she needs it more than I do.

"Why would I want to put my head on your shoulder?

I don't even know you," she says. Her hand is on the door, primed for a getaway.

I have said this out loud, I guess. My thoughts will sometimes not stay in my head, as hard as I try to keep them there, like this morning when I told Ray I was thinking about going back to the apartment in Durham. He talked to me all breezy-like, the way you talk to somebody you need to keep calm, whose head is spinning on its axis. He looked scared I was losing it again.

"Maybe that's the best reason to put your head on somebody's shoulder," I say.

We sit down on the wicker settee between the sink and the stall. Right by my head is a basket of cinnamon potpourri someone has put out to cover the smell of people's bowel movements, which tend to be worse in a place like this. The sweet and the spice and the stink together make me feel a little sick. I don't think it's doing Dolly any good, either.

"He told my boy Scottie I never wanted him," she says. "He told him about when we went to the clinic, but he left out the part about how I changed my mind at the last minute and made him turn the car around. That's how come Scottie wants to go live with him and that woman, that Suzanne."

She says the name like it's two separate words, *Su*

Zanne, and we agree that women named Suzanne are seldom to be taken at face value. I know, I work with one at the phone company. She doesn't like me because I complain about her electric pencil sharpener, how it's always grinding when I'm on the phone with customers. She really crams the pencils in there, like the sharpener's screwed with her somehow. Pretty sure she's the person who told on me that time I didn't clock out for lunch.

"But I realize that's not the point," I say.

Dolly sinks into the crook of my neck. Her smell puts me in this kind of Jean Naté haze that is a whole lot better than the bathroom's other haze. She gets so heavy and quiet on my arm that I think she's gone to sleep. After a while a tear rolls down my neck and across my chest, disappearing between my breasts. It warms me.

"I don't know what to do," she says. "I don't know what to do."

I thought I would come up with beautiful words of comfort just for her. People say I have a way with words. I've written three Tentacles songs, all of them about people leaving.

"You gotta hold on, you gotta safety-pin that heart, you gotta give all you got to give and then you gotta make a new start," I say. I'm quoting "Love Casserole," which won fourth place at Riv3rJ@m last year. The next line is

"Hope is the lonely voice in the heart of our despair," but that seems like it will only make things worse.

She goes all stiff in my arms. I've said the wrong thing.

"I ought to be getting back to my tables," she says. She gets up and fixes herself in the mirror, smoothing out her hair and retying her apron. When she sees me looking at her in the mirror, I imagine her life reassembling itself around her, Scottie, tables needing to be wiped down outside, the light bill past due. She sees me noticing all this, and she's embarrassed. The woman on the settee with the gold eyes that stare too long has tried to sell her a sackful of cat turds.

By the time she pulls the door open, the white Nashville teeth are out. She's Dolly again. I want to give her my phone number, tell her that she can call me any time she needs anything, even if it's just a cup of frozen yogurt in the middle of the night, but she's gone.

. . .

When I get back to our table, I feel like doing some damage to those who have damaged me. To Temple, who has eaten my creamed corn and spelled out "F U" in green beans on my plate. To Ray and Lionel, who are laughing, probably at that.

It must be twenty ounces of tea, ice and everything, that winds up on Temple's head. She jumps so high out of her chair that the guys have to use their butter knives to scrape her off the ceiling. When they've got her down, Lionel skootches all our napkins into one big wad and dabs at her hair, face, breasts. It was a large tea, so his hands move fast. I think about how fast they'd move if I'd had coffee instead. Temple's skin is swelling up good and mean, with an apricot blister shaped like South Carolina.

"I don't know, Ede, that wasn't cool," Ray says, probably thinking about the coffee version. The other people in our section are staring at us, cornbready mouths hanging open, probably upset that their slow drip of grease and friendly service has been pinched off for this.

Lionel tells Ray he should take me back to the hotel, straighten me out, which is the kind of thing he says when I do things.

I wait for Ray to tell Lionel to shove it, to tell him about Temple. He looks back and forth between them, making me wish I had another glass of tea. Since I don't, I tell them I'm taking the van. They sit there looking at me with their tentacles swirling around them, like I'm the one with the problem. I'm not. I'm the one with the keys to the van.

I want to get Temple's goat one last time. I decide to finish the pegboard game, just to drag this out. Nobody makes for the keys in my pocketbook; they just watch me, waiting for me to jump that last peg, waiting for me to explode. I make it last as long as I can. When Dolly comes back to refill our drinks, it's like nothing happened in the bathroom. I guess, as far as she's concerned, Temple doesn't have tea drizzling out of her hair, and Lionel isn't rubbing at her chest with wet napkins, making things worse. She's so cool, so waitress-like, that I start to think we didn't have our arms around each other. Ray could be right about my head spinning off. I don't answer when Dolly asks if there's anything we want because, if I'm honest with myself, I can't think of one thing.

The Water Goblin

1.

The girl's hair is getting long. Braid it like a pretzel, tight so it doesn't break apart during the day. Name her Abigail, a hardworking name for girls who like hedgehogs and pretending not to understand Czech. Tidy rooms and spelling books and rising at five to open the shop, one day lines up in front of the other. A life stretches out.

The water goblin has hundreds of teacups, travel souvenirs or ones he bought online. Copenhagen, Disney World, Royal Doultons shipped all the way from England. When do goblins go on vacation? How do they get internet service all the way down there in the river?

2.

When you break one of the teacups, replace it with another and dispose of the shards in the neighbors' trash. Unpretzel Abigail's hair at night and let it fan across the pillow, one wave for each year of her future.

"What a future it will be," you say. Say it in Czech so she knows what hope sounds like in the old tongue. You have spoken English much of your life, but sometimes, in moments like this, it doesn't have the right weight.

3.

In stories of the *vodnik*, the water goblin, a girl would go missing and the mother had to search for her. Depending on who told it, the story's braid was different. The goblin drowned the girl, or he just kept her locked up. Which was worse? He took her down into the river's cold muck where she had its baby, and when she tried to leave he cut the baby's head off. The girl found the head floating in the river, bobbing like an apple.

Abigail's fourteen and testing boundaries, same as you did at that age. Tell her the boundaries are there for a reason, so she doesn't fall off the edge of the earth. So goblins don't pull her underwater. You don't want to find her head in a river or the garbage or anywhere. You don't say the thing about the goblins out loud, but you think it.

"Relax, Mom," she says, as if one's troubles dried up when the muscles of the body loosened. She's started saying this like the American girl she is. You want to scream at her, but there are two older girls idling in a Volkswagen, listening.

4.

The *vodnik* doesn't like people touching his things. His house is packed with teacups with souls trapped under them, and they better not get out. He worked hard to drown them all, to catch them again.

The house teems with trapped souls. Every time you enter a room, another one's rapping on the porcelain, wanting loose. You want to help but you don't like the thought of those angry souls swirling around you, confused about who killed them, who let them out.

When he can't find the tiny cup from Istanbul for

drinking sweet, sweet coffee, he comes looking for you.

"I know you've been breaking them and throwing them out. What I want to know is why."

He says you're not going anywhere. Have you always been unable to leave? You remember going to a job, the little bakery you own downtown. You had to get up so damn early to open the place. You think you've driven the girl to gymnastics, to dentist appointments, but these could be memories the goblin placed in your head.

5.

There isn't money for one of you to move out, but you're going. You and the girl.

Put yourself between him and her. He says, "No, no, no, no, no," like you're holding the box cutter and he's holding the mail.

You go first, for all the good that does.

"You'll have to go through me," you say. So he does. The sound of you tearing like cardboard is terrible. The newspaper story leaves that detail out but gets hung up on the teacups, hundreds and hundreds of them carted out of there in boxes. People assume they're your teacups, adding insult to injury. You didn't drown anybody, you wanted to let them out.

Later, people will look for a missing thread, something to isolate the act from their own lives. A struggle over money. You'd wanted to take the girl back to the old country. Nothing *they* had to worry about. The neighbors don't fight over money, and they aren't from somewhere else. No language older than memory, nothing lost in the translation, *just a tragedy*. There are no piles of teacups in their houses making deathtraps of the stairwells. Kind of weird, if you ask them, but the whole thing is.

"You never know what's going on with people," they'll say, hugging their live children, shepherding them back into the houses. Thankful everyone they love is still breathing.

The Princess

When the princess was born, the courtiers pushed into the room, not giving the exhausted queen a moment to recover.

"Long live the future queen!" one of them said.

The older courtiers pushed through the crowd to get a look at the princess. They held to the old ways and didn't approve of gender equality, girls inheriting thrones and such nonsense. It only led to trouble. They put in their ear horns and listened as the child's name was read off by the lord chamberlain. As the queen labored, he'd scuttled between the birthing room and the outer hall, updating the court on her progress.

"Elizabetta Sophia Christina Alexandra Anastasia

Graciela Lucretia Ariadne Mildred Caroline," the chamberlain read from a scroll.

The old fogies pulled their horns out of their ears. They'd heard enough. Most of the names were foreign-sounding, the names of entertainers, none of which they held with. They didn't hold with the queen either, since she wasn't from their ranks.

"This cannot stand," they said.

"Shut up, old man. Get with the new scene," piped up some of the younger ones, whose fortunes came from industry, not birthright.

"Eh?" said the Forty-seventh Earl of Swampsbury. His hearing loss was congenital and he walked with a limp, as many in the room did. The old families had been interbreeding with one another for centuries, limiting the gene pool.

The young Marquess of Weaselback shoved the earl, who, being of weak constitution, fell onto the floor.

"You'll pay for that," the earl said, throwing down his gauntlet. People of his generation often still carried gauntlets in case the need to duel presented itself.

A civil war launched right there on the parquet floor of the royal birthing room. It wasn't pretty.

More than one hundred years later the fight was still going on, and no one could remember what they'd been fighting about. Taxes, market economics, something. The only verifiable fact was that in the early months of the war the king was decapitated, a lesson in the shortcomings of autocracy. It was a shame. The king wasn't a bad guy. Sickly with a hunchback, inbred like the rest of them, but he'd instituted universal free education for all the peasant youngsters. His head sat in a glass case in the town square, decomposing without dignity.

Before all that, something weird happened.

As the nobles slugged it out next to the queen's bed, the old ways against the new ways, tradition against the future, Beyonce against Scott Joplin, a ball of light rose from the young princess' bassinette. The light filled the room, driving the brouhaha out into the hall, and when it died out the princess had transformed into a wood thrush.

"Climb on my back, Mother," the wood thrush said.

"You've got to be kidding," said the queen, who'd just endured twenty-seven hours of childbirth.

The wood thrush turned into a pelican and scooped the queen up in her beak. As she was about to take flight, she looked back and saw the chamberlain standing there, looking forlorn. Being pretty sure he was her real father, she bent down to let him climb up behind the queen.

The family took off into the sky. From the air, they could see what a beautiful kingdom it was. There was the white castle surrounded by its neat gray wall, and then the village with its snug little houses and rosy-cheeked peasants leading cows to market. Beyond that, the checkerboard of farmland stretching as far as the Black Forest.

"Is this what the kingdom looked like from inside?" the pelican asked. The only frame of reference she had for anything was the room she was born in.

"No," the queen and the chamberlain said in unison. They'd seen many things given their station, but never the kingdom from this angle.

"Things always look different from the inside of a place," the queen said. "Remember that when you're anywhere, or you'll end up like them."

The war was raging below them. The pelican saw fires burning and cannons and tanks and things being rolled out from the armory. Waves of soldiers poured in from the countryside. The pelican wasn't sure if they'd joined by choice or been conscripted, but watching as they fell into two camps facing each other on the battlefield, she decided it probably didn't matter. Soon the farmland would be on fire, maybe even the forest which spread out in front of them. The fields would be gooey with blood and the soldiers' still-beating hearts would be ripped out. She flew over as much of the world as she could, trying to see the whole thing before it was gone.

II.

Dark Paradise
(A Go-Wherever Novella)

The date is August 4, 1892, when history records that you killed your parents with a hatchet. Somebody even wrote a song about it.

> *Lizzie Borden took an axe*
> *Gave her mother forty whacks.*
> *When she saw what she had done*
> *She gave her father forty-one.*

History almost never records things correctly—leaving facts out, flat-out making things up. Same with songwriting, it's impossible to get to the truth. Like when you interviewed your Latin teacher for the school newspaper. You were thirteen and asked questions you already knew the answers to. You told the story however you wanted.

> *Why did you decide to become an educator?*
> She answered, *So I could mold young minds.*
> You wrote, *So I could hold pork rinds.*

> *Why is it important that students study Latin?*
> She answered, *It will improve their understanding of the English language and its grammar and usage.*
> You wrote, *Latin will be the language of the ruling class, after the Vampyres have infiltrated the world's governments. Learn it or perish.*

You made up your own thing. You were the student editor and had the power. It's kind of like that.

Fact: Mrs. Highwater, the geography instructor, did not have a second head growing out of her stomach, and its name wasn't Edith, and it couldn't whistle *The Star Spangled Banner*.

Fact: Time and space are the same thing. If you don't whack somebody upside the head with a hatchet in the parlor, they aren't dead in it on Saturday, when you're all supposed to go to the flower show. The reverse is also true.

Fact: Each moment you remain alive carries an equal probability of annihilation, of being rendered nil. A matter/antimatter explosion off your port bow.

Sometimes you practice feeling annihilated, standing very still and holding your breath, thinking things like *cosmic broth*, which is where you think the pieces of things go when they aren't things anymore. When you do this, people freak out.

"Lizzie? Lizzie? Lizzie?" they say, as if saying a person's name will shake them awake.

During these times they look at each other on the sly, trading facts about you with glances. This is how they ask each other, "Where does she go when she leaves like that?" You wish you knew.

. . .

The house on Second Street is a hot locked box you can't get out of. There's a triple-locked front door and bolts on all the bedroom doors for protection. The Old Man wants to keep everything valuable in the house, including you. He has frenemies.

For you, living in the house is like watching the world from inside a museum, everything sealed tight and nailed down. To get to one room you have to pass through another. There aren't any hallways you could use as escape routes, just a rabbit warren of rooms circling you back to the beginning. You're always passing through doorways, busting in on people in their skivvies.

Also, it's hot as hell in the house. The Old Man won't let you open any windows, which he says is like asking someone to sneak in and rob you blind.

"This house is hot as hell," you say.

"Lizzie Borden," your sister Emma says, but she's hot as hell too. Her armpits are waxing crescent moons.

You wish you'd gotten a couple of fans from the hardware store. You could have gotten one under your skirt, easy. There were other things: pots of skin cream from the pharmacy, hairpins, apricots, a pair of silk drawers. You had the money for all of it. Your natural klepto itch has you going for big things lately, like the fan. One day the stolen things will add up to a new life, and a new house will spring up in the old one's place. You're going to live in it.

"You mustn't steal, Lizzie," Emma says. "It's like a sin. Promise?"

Emma is as good as gold. Gooder than. At her center is a sugared raisin that grows sweeter by the year. The Old Man says it was in your mother, too. You have nothing soft and sweet in the center, just a space where the dark thoughts pile up. Still, you swear to get things honest from now on, to not go jacking people right and left. You promise to pay for everything one way or another.

The day you don't steal the fans from the hardware store, there's a blowup about the hot locked box, how you and Emma are suffocating in it.

The Old Man says, "No way we're moving. The house is fine."

He's getting to be an old geezer, and as he ages his fist gets tighter. He claims a dollar doesn't go as far as it used to.

"Nobody *needs* indoor plumbing," he says. He doesn't care that half the city has flush toilets and water gushing out of spigots in the wall. Think of the waste! "If all your friends jumped off a cliff, would you do it, too?"

"It's 1892, Ebenezer," you say. Not your best moment.

"You guys are driving me crazy," The Old Man says.

You just want to live on a quiet street without the spindles in the textile mills whirring in your head night and day. You want a clean, well-lighted place to do your business.

You used a toilet once. You'd called on Thomasina Gravelock to collect donations for the church rummage sale. It was glorious sitting on the little seat and watching your pee swirl into the void. You thought, *this is what nothingness is.* Tommie showed her potty off proudly, like she'd given birth to it. There will never be a potty in this house as long as your father's alive. You're a Borden, for crying out loud, the oldest money there is, and look how you live: kerosene lamps when everyone else has gas, going to bed at 7 o'clock in the winter to save fuel. It's enough to fill you with a righteous rage.

"I'm filled with a righteous rage!" you say.

"What are you even talking about?" The Old Man says. "I give you guys an allowance. You can do anything you want with it. Take a trip, have a python shipped from the Amazon, for all I care."

Send off for the python out of spite. Set it up with a terrarium and what have you. The day it arrives, it will get out and swallow the maid and one of the kids next door. The child will be rescued, but the maid, who is further down the snake's gullet, will die waiting to get saved.

Tell the python story later in life when people are getting on your nerves. It's a lie, but tell it anyway. Whether they believe you or not, a piece of the puzzle will snap into place, in which you're a person who kept a python in her house or was just willing to lie about it. When you talk about the python, they'll step out of arm's reach of you. They'll stop asking you things.

• • •

Fact: You don't get along with your stepmother.

Correction: You don't make an attempt to get along with your stepmother.

Correction: You go out of your way not to get along with your stepmother. You and Emma were doing fine, raising yourselves when she came along, which is why you call her Mrs. Borden. She isn't your mother.

Your stepmother's the superstitious type, throwing salt over her shoulder and blessing every sneeze. She believes a person's soul can escape through their nostrils. Turn this like a rusty key.

Fifty years ago in the house next door, your cousin Eliza up and drowned her three children in the cistern well and then cut her own throat. Tell your stepmother about it because it's what's about to happen turned inside out.

"Don't speak of such things, Lizzie," she says. "If I ever lost you and Emma..."

The Old Man says you have to get along with your stepmother. He's had enough of the pranks, the stealing. He reminds you that you're a Borden. Remind him that the story of cousin Eliza is true and he was alive then. You aren't making up the bangs and giggles, and you didn't start the rumor about the bottom of the well being a hole the children fell straight through to another world, where they grew up and all went into the insurance industry.

"Kill me. You guys are killing me," he says.

When you're grown up, don't speak directly to your stepmother, to tell her a ghost story or anything. Pass messages through the maid. It's another locked door in the house, another wall holding you in the hot box.

• • •

You know how it sounds. Any way you look at it, you sound like a jerk. But it isn't like that. All your life you've been cooped up in that box, no hallways to escape through. Then a few weeks before everything changes, Mrs. Borden gets a letter in the mail.

Your stepmother has a younger half-sister, Sarah, who's your age, your step-half-aunt, who she could have been off mothering instead of you. The letter says the sister's landlord is kicking her out, and unless The Old Man helps she'll be on the street.

"She's not moving in here," you say.

All you want is a house of your own you can breathe in, mess around in. You'd haunt the crap out of it, like the white mist children on the staircase. You know there's enough money to make ghosts of you and Emma.

The Old Man waves the deed to the half-sister's house.

"The deed is done," he says. "Ha ha!"

He's bought the damn house.

"He's bought the damn house!" you tell Emma. It's not a big house or in a good part of town, but still.

Emma's mouth is open a little. She's about to take a breath and hold it, like when she walks across bridges, a precaution to get her to the other side alive. She watches the empty space inside you expand, her eyes harvest moons as she waits for the explosion.

. . .

Follow your stepmother up to the guest room, where she's making up the bed. Ask if she needs any help. Don't linger in the doorway like a weirdo or she'll suspect something.

"Lizzie, dear, you startled me," she says. She startles easy, another key you like to turn.

You think of Mrs. Borden as always making up a bed. She fights the good fight against disarray, tucking sheets under mattresses so when you get in bed you're a letter sliding into an envelope. She must do other things in the house, but you can't think of what. You mostly pretend she doesn't exist.

You've always wondered why she and your father had no children. She was still young when they married. Was there a missing piece that kept a baby from holding on, like the hole inside you? Or was the defect on the outside? *Abby Borden is a plain but not bad-looking woman*, people say. They also say a woman over thirty is more likely to be struck by lightning than to find a husband. She must have been relieved when The Old Man came along.

"Before you married The Old Man, were you afraid of being struck by lightning? Did you worry about being annihilated?"

You want to explain how close you are to death every minute, that forces are working against you in the universe, how life is one improbable mystery continually unfolding, but the hatchet hidden in your skirt is cutting into your leg.

"I never know what you mean, dear," Mrs. Borden says. "Good grief, help me straighten this duvet."

*

Go to Fury *(Pg. 179)*
or Emma *(Pg. 202)*

Emily Koon

Fury

The song will talk about an axe, but you'll kill them with a hatchet.

You got the idea from a man in a traveling circus you saw as a child. He threw hatchets at his partner. He said he loved the woman, Esmeralda, who stood straight as an arrow against the wall, trusting him to hit the X over her head.

"If I did not trust my own skill, would I allow her to stand there, the mother of my children?" he said.

He was asking the audience's permission, showing them what he loved by risking its annihilation. If he missed, it would be their fault.

Emma ran out of the tent then. She couldn't handle the thought of the woman's forehead splitting open, brains flying. You had to drag her to the circus because The Old Man wouldn't let you go alone, and, at seventeen, Emma was already a recluse, sewing herself up inside the house. You stayed until the end of the show hoping to see the woman's head split like a melon. You went back every day for the next week, but the man always hit the X.

Emma's gone to Fairhaven for the week. You weren't invited, and now you're alone. Not really, but sort of. No one has spoken directly to anyone else all day. You've all been passing messages through Bridget, the maid. *Ask Lizzie to post my letter when she goes to the pharmacy. Tell Mrs. Borden I am ill again.*

This morning you heard Mrs. Borden call you her daughter, though she has none. *Your womanhood has come to naught,* you want to yell to her, but you don't because so has yours. At thirty-two, you're still sealed tight. If you could feel sorry for her, you'd let this pass.

Tell her through Bridget, "We're all out of butter." She should know you mean, "My mother is dead." There is an ache. To watch her all these years wearing your mother's skin, stretching it out with her stout frame, was too much. The prosecutor will draw a line between this and the two bodies, your father with his face hacked to ground beef, your stepmother with her skull poured out.

Use the hatchet after the poison has failed and you end up with a houseful of sick stomachs to tend. Such is life, such is death.

"Your stepmother has to go first or you and Emma won't get squat," the Thing says. "You won't be destitute, mind you, but you won't have flush toilets either. It's up to you."

The Thing has a wide half-moon smile full of tall yellow teeth and takes the shape of other people. When it's in the basement, it's cousin Eliza. Those times it warns you there will be a fire or another terrible, terrible accident and you're the only one who can stop it. It warns you to stay away from wells.

"Destitution is in the eye of the beholder," you say.

Ask the Portuguese factory women with their babies strapped to them in slings, being ground down, what enough is. Ask anyone who is richer or poorer than anyone else. You want to not have to piss in a bucket. You want a bedroom door you don't have to bolt. You're more afraid of what's in the house than what's outside it.

Sometimes you think the Thing is just your thoughts—the dark center where your raisin should be. Sometimes it has a form, climbing into bed with you at night, making you sleep with two pairs of drawers on. Sometimes you think there is no Thing, that it's you, and you just made it up so when something bad happens you have someone to blame. It's possible the Thing is all these things.

Wait for the right moment, when she's turned toward the window. Don't bring the hatchet out until the little hand is on the nine and the big one's on the twenty. At thirty, she'll go down for the mail.

Mrs. Borden startles easy, like she thinks a spook's come down the chimney. She's sort of right. There are a lot of spooks in this house. The Thing, cousin Eliza, you. She'll be the kind that makes up beds. You'll walk into a room to find it's tidied itself, towels folded, clothes put away, the best kind of ghost to have.

"Stand away from the window so the Thing can take your head off," you say.

"I never know what you mean, dear," she says. "Good grief, help me straighten this duvet."

When people ask questions, tell them you only held the door open for the Thing. As far as they know, you were just straightening the duvet.

Pull the duvet as tight as it will go. Pull so hard the opposite corner flies out of your stepmother's hands.

"Mercy, Lizzie," she'll say. Her blood will end up all over you.

Mrs. Borden goes down easy. One whack to open her skull, one for wanting you to call her Mother, the rest for everything else. Your father's face slides off like a fried egg out of the pan.

• • •

Tell this story at the inquest:

1. You're in the kitchen ironing handkerchiefs when The Old Man comes home with a sick stomach. He works like some men drink, but today he needs little coaxing to lie down on the settee in the parlor and rest. Roll up his jacket to make a pillow for him, and once he's closed his eyes, go back to the kitchen. You won't hear the Thing crawl out of its hiding place and slice his face off.

Don't say the last part to the judge.

2. You're upstairs when your father comes home. Somehow you don't see your stepmother on the guest room floor, congealing plain as day. Everyone else sees her from the top of the stairs, but your mind's been on other things. How hot it is. How the cistern well is a black hole in the earth with no bottom, that any thing or person could fall into.

3. You're in the barn when your father is killed. It's August and hotter than the dickens. In the barn you can't smell the others, their layers of sweat and distrust, their despair, their interpersonal crap, over the thousand barn odors.

You eat two pears in spite of your own sick stomach. A weird place to eat pears, even hotter and darker than the house. It's why you don't have any blood on you when they look. Whoever kills your father jumps down the well after they're done and takes the hatchet with them.

. . .

"What were you doing in the barn?" the prosecutor wants to know.

He's been crawling around you like a ferret looking for holes to slip through.

"Eating pears," you say. "A few had fallen off the tree, so I had to eat them up."

"That doesn't make any sense."

"I don't care if makes sense or not. It's nothing to me."

"What in the devil were you doing in that barn?"

You already told him you were eating pears.

"It was too hot to be inside a windowless barn eating pears, and you've already testified that you felt sick that morning. You'd all been sick that morning."

It wasn't because you tried to poison anybody. It wouldn't have made sense, poisoning yourself, which is why you poisoned yourself a little bit, too.

"I felt well enough to eat the pears," you say.

"It doesn't follow that you were in that barn eating pears. Any reasonable person would have been sitting in the shade of the pear tree itself, not mucking around in a hot barn."

You're not a reasonable person, anyone can see that.

. . .

Wear black to the trial to appear distraught. Your lawyer says juries operate on sympathy and won't convict anyone they pity, which is why he calls you *this girl*. You are thirty-two years old.

Bring roses to mask the smell of people's unwashed places in the courtroom. Bring them up to your nose when the testimony gets rough, laying the groundwork for a fainting spell. The newspapers will write that your behavior is a sign of grief. Maybe the man typing what everyone says on the little machine will put it into the record.

Miss Borden covered her face in grief. Grief annihilates culpability.

"This girl," your lawyer starts every sentence.

This girl is

This girl never

This girl could not
This girl, whom we all know,
This girl embodies everything

You embody everything that is good about America. You're a woman of values and tradition. You think of your body as a circle, bound by your skin, housing all that is good in the world. There wasn't room for the Thing to crawl in and do *that awful business*, what you call the murders. So, when Mr. Knowlton, the prosecutor, unwraps the skulls of The Old Man and Mrs. Borden, it's not an act that you faint.

You didn't know they were buried without their heads. Why didn't anyone tell you? Your lawyer explains that the prosecution needed to test the hatchets in front of the jury, so they sawed them right off.

"They wanted to see if they fit," he says. "To see if the murder weapon was one of the hatchets from the house."

"Did any of them?" you ask. "Was it?"

You make your face like the face of someone who doesn't know the answer to a question.

*

Go to Three Hundred Thousand *(Pg. 187)*
or Down a Well *(Pg. 215)*

Three Hundred Thousand

Lizzie Borden took an axe, gave her mother forty whacks.

No one has ever been able to prove this. Probably because the song contains a lie: your mother was actually your stepmother, proof this was all a mix-up.

Your friend Nance O'Neil thinks so. She wants to write a play about your life, how you stuck it to the legal system. She's been on your side since after the trial, when newspapers shouted your liberation.

Lizzie Free.

You're so famous now, you don't need a last name, like Cher.

Lizzie Borden Not Guilty.

Not the same thing as saying you're innocent, you explain to Nance, who claims to believe in you.

"Nobody's innocent," you say, to Nance and anyone else who says you are. Not very many people.

Nance is the new it girl, the actress everyone's talking about. You meet her in Boston after the trial, when home starts feeling too small. The haters in Fall River don't welcome you in their society, so you find your own. New York, Boston, you do what you want. Life is meant to be lived, a journey into the unknown. A corner of the world is peeled back to show colors you never saw in Fall River. Brownstone, blackjack, limelight. On Second Street, all you wanted was to mix with the right sort, so of course you mix with the wrong sort now. You're drawn to actors, musicians, artists, people who play cards for a living.

Imagine yourself a musician, playing Bach in the Boston Music Hall. You'd have been a violist because all your life until now has been a harmony running quietly under the melody, being overlooked until a moment came to break out.

• • •

The new house you buy for you and Emma, that you spend less and less time at as the years go by, is a big sprawling thing. The house is big and airy with proper hallways separating the sections, and whole days roll by that you never see Emma. You call the house Maplecroft because it makes you think of open farmland scattered with orange-haired trees in fall, sap dripping from the trunks. The Old Man used to take you to the family farm in Swansea when you were younger. There must have been maple trees there; you and Emma must have made bonnets out of their leaves.

You're able to afford Maplecroft because of what was hiding inside the Union Savings Bank after The Old Man died. *Three hundred thousand.* When his lawyer, Mr. Jennings, brought the papers over, you had to write it out as words. You knew there was a lot, but dang. It helped that The Old Man never modernized the house, that you had to use the slop pail when girls below your station had flush toilets. If The Old Man had ever gone on the rag, water pipes would have vined the insides of the walls.

If The Old Man had ever gone on the rag, the whole history of the world would have been different.

. . .

After the trial, everything comes to you and Emma. You made sure of that.

"What will we do with three hundred thousand dollars?" Emma asks.

She can't get her mouth around the number any more than you can. She worried you'd be bag ladies, now she worries about spending it all.

"Anything you want," Mr. Jennings says. "Take a trip, have a python shipped in from the Amazon, whatever."

Someone spills the beans about how much you've inherited. Headlines shout *three hundred thousand. Hun thoured threesome.* On your way to the bank to sign the papers, a woman on the street gets in your face about it, a sign of things to come.

"The famous Lizzie Borden," she says. You're already a legend in your own time. "I hadn't thought you killed them for so much."

How much should you have killed them for?

• • •

You aren't welcomed into society, but that's all right. On Second Street, you and Emma had formed your own society, your dreams peopling its roads and houses and churches.

You had that dream where the house was a flying machine. You bought flying goggles, turned the crank in the back and said, "Where to, Miss?" and a few minutes later were on a beach. The beach was holding a festival with a Ferris wheel and a tattooed woman eating fire.

How is it possible to eat fire? How would a person would even think about doing that? There are things in the world even your mind can't invent.

"You have to imagine yourself as the fire," the fire eater said. "That's the trick. The rest is just swallowing."

The woman opened her mouth and became the fire.

Even her tongue was tattooed, with, what else, a lick of flame. Eventually, her body burned off. She was nothing more than a shimmer melting into the flames, and you saw how she'd done it. She'd eliminated the barrier between the fire and herself.

Emma rode the Ferris wheel but didn't like the fire eater, like at the circus when you were a child and she wouldn't stay to see if the hatchet thrower hit his mark. The only way she allowed herself to let go, to become fire, was when she walked to the edge of the water and lifted her skirt so it was above the foam. Her ankles had never had the sun on them. You couldn't remember seeing Emma's ankles before, even in the house.

"Mine haven't seen the sun before either," you said, seeing that she was embarrassed. You both hitched up your skirts and let the sea air kiss your skin. Later you rubbed aloe on each other's sunburned ankles and felt what it was like to be fire.

. . .

Emma only asks you about the murders once. Was there was a chance you could have done it, maybe without knowing?

"You know how sometimes you go all quiet and still,"

she says.

She means how you practice being annihilated, and this backfires and you end up splitting into two people, the good Lizzie who teaches Sunday School and the bad Lizzie whose soul is a rotted-out hole, who *does things*. You think it's possible for a person to live out separate destinies at the same time. Sometimes you wake up in a different dress than you recall putting on, sometimes weeks later, and don't remember anything that's happened. Once you woke up and the house had been painted a different color, a terrible mushroom brown. When you asked about it, they said you'd chosen the color.

You remember a hatchet in your hands, though. It cut through the air in an arc shape, a body in motion acting on a body at rest, the force equaling the mass of the hatchet times acceleration. How do you figure out the acceleration?

You seemed to be moving forward, but what if you're not remembering it right? What if you're not remembering backwards but forwards? As far as you know, time is laid out the same way space is, one thing next to another, in which case you can move in either direction. Unless there's no time, unless everything's happening at once, and your brain's just teasing it out this way.

"Everything's happening all at once," you say.

"I feel sick. I'm going to lie down," Emma says.

Emma needs to get out of the house. She's killing you with her needlework. Embroidery is the gateway drug, the road to Shut-In Town, the thing old women stitch hours together with to make them pass. Warn her to live a little.

"Go on, Lizzie. I'm happy here in the house," she says.

You aren't happy in the house. You don't know how anyone can be. It's why you spend weeks at a time in Boston, fooling around with Nance and them.

"We didn't claw our way out of Dad's house just to hole up in this dump," you say.

"Lizzie Borden. This house cost a pretty penny."

You know what it cost.

"Wasn't it you who wanted to live among the fashionable set? Wasn't it you who wanted a flush toilet?" she says.

To flush secrets down, yes.

The house has two cans, one for each of you. They're bottomless like the cistern well at the old house. Some days you never get off yours. You go and flush and wait until the need arises again. You never get tired of watching your waste spiral down the hole. Everything about the trial and the Thing is eventually flushed down it, and you never see it again.

Boredom makes you steal again. First it's little things, such as fingernail files and handfuls of screws from the hardware store. Eventually you get brave again and stow the tragedies of William Shakespeare in your jacket. When you speak to them in the shops, the other ladies don't meet your gaze. Maybe it's because they know what's in your jacket, maybe it's because of your eyes, which everyone says are piercing. You don't think it's a compliment. There's this feeling when you talk to people that they're holding their breath, waiting for you to explode.

. . .

Nance has taken to calling you Lizzie Morbid lately. You've sung her the rhyme children sing when they ring your doorbell and run away—*Lizzie Borden took an axe*—and she's made her own game out of it.

"Lizzie Morbid's skates make tracks..."

She's skating circles around you on the iced-over pond on Boston Common.

"That's not funny, Nance. It was an awful time in everyone's life."

"Not mine," she says. "I was living in New York, drinking champagne and kissing boys."

Nance loves you, but she can be a big old witch,

saying things like that. You wouldn't trade her, not even for Emma's sake would you send her away (now that you've experienced life apart from Emma, you realize how thin the ribbon binding the two of you is), but sometimes you see Nance under the ice, struggling for air. The day she tells you she's engaged to Alfred, you sink to all fours on the ice and wipe away the frost made by crisscrossed skate tracks. There's Nance's face under the surface, her lips a cold blue, one bloodless hand pushing against the ice.

"Nance, get out of the water. It's January, you nuts?" you say.

She skates another circle around you. Your body is a circle inside a circle inside a circle, containing the whole history of everything. If you aren't careful, the circle will collapse and everything you've done to get here will unravel.

"What are you barking about?" Nance says, dry and bundled in a fox coat, her lips painted persimmon.

"I thought you were dead," you say. "I thought I'd killed you."

"Queer girl."

Invite your city friends to visit you in Fall River. Bring them to Maplecroft to show Emma they're good people, even though some of them aren't. (Wilfred shoplifts like you, and Rufus and Mildred live together but are both married to other people. What Emma doesn't know won't hurt her.) You haven't gotten her to join you on a single trip to Boston or New York. It's a waste of freedom, provided by a house that isn't a hot locked box. When you speak of your friends, she can't keep them straight.

"She's the actress? He's the one who had a career as a tightrope walker? Who's the one who fell out of the boat into the Charles River?"

The last time you bring them, before you don't ever see Emma again, Rufus and Mildred drink a case of champagne in a weekend. They put on *A Midsummer Night's Dream* in the yard, and later Humphrey organizes a wedding between two of the dogs.

He says, "We are here to join Franklin and Albertine in mari-tail bliss."

"It's cute how your sister calls you Lizzie," says Nance. You go by Lizbeth now because Lizzie sounds like something you'd call a child, and you are definitely not a child.

"It's her name," Emma says. She will not look directly at Nance.

. . .

Emma moves out of the house in 1905. You'd disappeared

after New Year's when a progressive dinner in Hartford, Connecticut stretched out for twenty-three days and you didn't so much as send a telegram.

"I don't know you anymore," she says. "These people in Boston. This is what you wanted off Second Street for?"

The older you get, the more you think about when you were children. After your mother died, before The Old Man married your stepmother, Emma took care of you. The nine years between you were enough to feel safe only with her, for her to mind you as a little mother. Little Mother became your name for her.

You never see Emma again, but there are a handful of letters over the years. She buys a house in New Hampshire that doesn't have a name and breaks her hip the same day you die. She dies a few weeks after that, like the ribbon between you has been cut.

. . .

Nance has become famous, unbearably so. In 1917, she stars in one of those "movie" things, similar to a play being acted out on a screen. You don't understand the magic that makes it work, but the pictures actually move, as people say. Nance's movie is a murder mystery called *Dark Paradise*. You knew when you told her the story she would use it one day, and you're all over the screen, the high-necked dresses, the hatchet, the pears. Nance gets top billing playing you.

A few days after the opening you're on the third page of the *Boston Globe,* coming out of the theater with Nance. The way your mouth hangs open, you look like you've had a stroke. The headline reads, *Nance O'Neil's new film opens to acclaim. Companion Lizzie Borden looks none too pleased with it.*

They still call you her *companion,* like you're a couple of old ladies. You suspect they mean something else. Fortunately for you, in May the Germans sink the *Lusitania* and no one cares who Nance is running around with.

You hope Emma doesn't see the movie. She wouldn't like herself in it, the gooder-than-gold sister who stood in the background and let things happen. You remember the day before that awful business, when she held her breath, waiting for what came next. Somehow they've put this in the movie, the moment before you broke your promise to be good, when her eyes were harvest moons.

Nance has broken trust with you, like you have with Emma. You probably deserve it. It still hurts that the heroine in the movie is a killer, not innocent like Nance always said. What does it say about Nance that she believes you are guilty but is your friend anyway? Not that you can judge, but still.

"There wouldn't be a movie otherwise," she says. "No one wants to hear a story about a decent person." She thinks people have probably forgotten your story, which is ten years old now, like a child you raised. "If anyone does remember, they don't care," she says.

That's when you find out Nance doesn't have a raisin either.

. . .

You haven't had a letter from Emma in three years.

"After all I sacrificed, all I did to make her happy," you say.

"I don't know what that means," Nance says.

You've never told her.

In her last letter, Emma talked about a shell garden she made in front of her new house. Scallops, whelks, olives and murex are arranged in the beds instead of flowers, which would just die on her. She mostly wanted to know about the dogs.

> *How are Albertine and Teddy and the others? Has Marcel's skin condition cleared up? I think often*

of them running back and forth across the porch, barking at squirrels, and wonder if I ought not get a dog myself. I just have this parakeet, which I call Lizzie because I find myself talking to it in the way I once talked to you. She's a thief, too. Anyway, how are the dogs?

You didn't have the heart to tell her most of the dogs were dead. By then the only one you had left was Harold, and he was twelve years old. It's when you realized Emma had been gone ten years. In your last letter, you sent an old photo of the dogs and signed all their names at the bottom of the letter next to little ink pawprints. What was the harm? She wasn't coming back. In the letter you wrote,

Little Mother,

I think often of death, how your leaving was a kind of annihilation. I fear I'll never see you again, that you'll die in your bed and no one will tell me for years and years. I think worse things than that, that you are somehow disappointed in me, after everything that's happened. Mass times acceleration equals a raisin, what you call love. Can you not see how all of this was for you?

You shouldn't have expected a reply, but each day you look for one.

. . .

After *Dark Paradise* opens, the New England Society of Theater and Film Arts gives Nance an award. In his introduction, the chairman says she's the next Lillian Gish, better than Sarah Bernhardt, even. You think she was better on the stage, when she wasn't this famous. She didn't think she'd ever *be* famous, so it was just about the work. Now she's up on a dais, accepting a piece of silver shaped like a naked body, holding it to her heart to applause that rumbles the room.

The clip they play from the movie is the one where she runs onto a beach in a thunderstorm, chased by a police captain who's in love with her. It's Nance at what you call *peak Nance*: hysterical, bottom lip trembling, hair streaming out of its bun like octopus tentacles, her eyes dark pits of love and despair. She forces the world to rotate around her center, waiting for her to explode. She has drawn you to her. You allowed yourself to be pulled out of the other orbit you were in like this happens every day; bodies changing allegiances, seduced by the larger thing's gravity. Maybe it does happen every day. You haven't heard from Emma since you don't know when.

The heroine of *Dark Paradise* is guilty, but other details are different. Nobody puts anything down a well. The killer hides the murder weapon in the maid's room, and it's an axe just like in the song. You think if Nance was going to steal your story, she could at least have gotten it right.

*
Go to Dark Paradise (Pg. 229)
or Dissolution (Pg. 224)

Emma

If Emma hadn't been standing here looking at you like that, like you were about to blow a gasket, would things have turned out differently? You knew what she was thinking. The hole in you where the raisin should be isn't a stable circle. It expands, and she's learned to read the warning signs. Right before it opens up and engulfs everything, there's always intense pressure, so much that you feel time slowing down. You hear the warped voices of the people in the room as if they're speaking to you underwater. You feel yourself being stretched, your head pulled one way and your feet the other, until you're a string of particles falling into the hole along with everything else that is or has ever happened, as far back as the beginning of the universe. In that moment, you disappear. You stop talking mid-sentence. You stand up and look around the room as if you've never seen it before. Your eyes glass over like a person who's died, and sometimes it's days, weeks before you're right again.

Emma never disappears like that. She can't look into the past like you can. She can't remember the future. She deals with the hot locked box by accepting it, sewing herself up in the house, which is why you have to get her out of it.

Think about your promise not to steal. You haven't. You haven't done anything to anyone, and this means something, like you can look at the line formed by the edge of the street and not walk across it into traffic. You have a choice in what happens to you next.

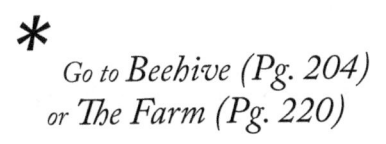

*
*Go to Beehive (Pg. 204)
or The Farm (Pg. 220)*

The Beehive

After the business with the half-sister, The Old Man has no choice but give in on the new house. You give him hell, listing off the whys until he's worn down:

1. Ghosts—The house is full of them. Some are people and others are just bad smells and memories. You want to live in a house where nothing horrible has happened. Your mother is a ghost living in your stepmother's body, and anyone can see that's not right.

2. Everything else.

"Mother would have wanted it this way," you say.

The Old Man complains there's an air of conspiracy, that the women in his house are ganging up on him, even the dead ones.

"I just want one sweet moment of peace before I up and die!" he says.

Ask for the big yellow house on French Street, and

when it's bought name it The Beehive because, with its three gingerbread verandas stacked on top of each other, that's what it reminds you of. He'll throw up his hands and say, "Whatever, I'm tired," and sign the papers. There's one floor for you, one for Emma, and one for them, so you hardly see each other.

. . .

The Old Man and your stepmother never settle into the new house. They can't get comfortable in the big, drafty rooms. All they see is waste: space and stuff and time. After a few weeks, they're tired from so much inside walking.

"We're too old for so much house," says Mrs. Borden.

"I regret this. I regret all of this," The Old Man says. He gets into the carriage and, sticking a grizzled hand out the window (everything about him is grizzled, even his hands), waves the house and everything in it away. You and Emma are standing on the porch. "Do whatever. I could care less," he says.

They float back to Second Street with the ghosts.

. . .

There's something not right about the house. Everyone

says so. Andrew Borden, known codger, would not have bought a house like that, not even for his girls. At the library fundraiser, your first social event since leaving Second Street, Jeremiah Potter has a possible answer.

"Maybe there's a rip in space-time and we've all fallen into the hole," he says.

Jeremiah subscribes to science magazines and always has one rolled up and sticking out of his coat pocket. He also stutters the first word of every sentence. These are the only solid facts you know about him. Other than the fact that you're in love with him. When he talks about kinetograms and electromagnetic radiation, he may as well be proposing.

He mentions an article he read, about how space and time are one thing and the thing can be torn like fabric, leaving gaps. It's a new theory, that space and time need each other to exist. Otherwise, everything just kind of piles up.

"Time moves forward because the universe tends toward disorder," he says. "It's why you can only move forward and only see backward. It runs in a line created by our choices, which create the disorder."

Because people are flawed, clumsy idiots. He says if there is a hole in space-time, some kind of explosion or anomaly altering the fabric, all bets are off.

You're not sure about the only moving forward part, but you like the thought of time being created by you, of space opening up across the years of your life, making room for things to happen.

The rip is possible because of your cousin Eliza4';;;/ and those poor children down the well. Maybe somebody's put you down one? If that's true, what are you supposed to do? You have a life to live here, wherever/whenever here is. You decide to move forward, put one foot in front of the other, because it is possible to do so.

The first thing you do is set up a beehive out back, a miniature version of the house, which is a miniature of the world you're living in down the well. A few months later, a box of bees comes in the mail. Emma reads you the pamphlet that comes with them, showing how to care for them and the different bees' jobs in the colony.

"This one here's the queen. She's the most important," she says.

The queen is bigger than the other bees, with long stained glass wings that beat up and down when she gives orders. The pamphlet says she's called The Bride because it will be her job to mate. You wonder if this is considered degrading in the bee universe. Does the queen choose her own mates, or is it like with most of the people you know? If you and Jeremiah Potter were bees, would he mate with you or be off in the honeycomb, reading science magazines? Because you and Emma never had suitors, you don't have a frame of reference.

You should be happy, but you're not. You have independence, your own hive to run, a maid, and a groundskeeper who builds the little house for your bees. But you think it can all slip away from you. Even though The Beehive is two miles from Second Street, there's the feeling that you haven't really left. An invisible thread connects the two front doors, and any minute you could be pulled back.

The New Bedford attorney you see under the alias of Miss Kitty Weathercock says the rug could be pulled out from under you, easily. You've rummaged through The Old Man's things and haven't found a will. What's going to happen to you? What's going to happen to Emma, the only person in the world you love (if love is what a person without a raisin at their center feels for someone else)?

"If I were you, I'd be hoping my stepmother took a little tumble down the stairs, if you know what I mean," the attorney says.

You know what he means. He knows you know. He doesn't have a raisin either.

• • •

You're welcomed into society, finally. When they visit, people say what they've been thinking all these years.

"It was a shame, that house. No running water and all. However did you wash?"

Of all the things about your life on Second Street, people are most curious about that. How does a person get clean without running water to carry the filth off? When the Thing visited you, you had to wash several times a day. All those stairs between the basement and your bedroom. Your knees ached later.

"We managed, didn't we, Emma? We had a spigot in the basement," you say.

"It wasn't so bad," she says, making a face. She doesn't like it when you talk about spigots.

A school friend of Emma's named Mrs. Violet Buttermill takes a minute to process, probably thinking of poop and sweaty armpits.

"Mercy," she finally says, sipping her tea.

"I expect you've never shat in a bucket in your whole life," you say.

"I don't know as I have," she says. She swats a bee from her sugar cube.

There are two bees buzzing around in here. Any minute one of them will sting her and she'll go. You've found this is a good way of getting rid of people.

"I have always preferred Darjeeling, myself," Mrs. Buttermill adds.

She's answering a comment Emma has made about tea, not what you've said about the bucket. You've said it in your head. The bee sting leaves a welt in the shape of a heart on her arm.

• • •

Emma needs to get out more. You're afraid she's turning into a cat. Try to get her out in the community, party like it's 1899. She's mostly quiet during visits from the Gravelocks and the Buttermills and the other Bordens, who are all related to each other many times over. Double, triple, quadruple cousins. How many generations before the disfigurements start? Doesn't your cousin Catherine's boy have a harelip?

"Go on, Lizzie," Emma says. "I'm good chillaxing here in the house."

You aren't happy in the house, you don't want to chillax. The bees get inside and sting you, and the stings carry messages. *Go to the pharmacy and put a package of hairpins up your sleeve.* You want to get rid of the hive, but no one will come get it. How do you run off bees?

"Quit chillaxing, quit embroidering. We didn't claw

our way out of Dad's house just to hole up in this dump," you say.

"Lizzie! This house cost a pretty penny. Wasn't it you who wanted to live among the fashionable set? Wasn't it you who wanted a flush toilet?" Emma says.

To flush regrets down, yes.

Give up on Emma when she's being a cat. Call on one of your school friends, sort cans at the church food pantry, attend garden parties and teas, even if the society ladies are boring as turnips. Living on Second Street, you thought they must have been doing interesting things with their time. There were suffrage events to organize. There was champagne to sip. Maybe one or two dabbled in the dark arts, huddled around Ouija boards. The thing they talk about most is garments. How many they have, where best to acquire more, what solutions their maids use to get stains out of them.

Maybe their domestic natter is code for something. Like, by *embroider a handkerchief*, they mean *take a lover*. By *have a game of lawn tennis*, they mean *tunnel into the bank*. You listen for patterns, possible substitutions hinting at a secret world, but you can't break the code because there's nothing to break. They're boring rich women, and you're one of them now.

• • •

The Old Man keeps a key to the house to remind you he owns it, owns you, and it can all be pulled out from under you. Every time you have the locks changed, the locksmiths send him a copy. Andrew Borden made Fall River's lock business what it is, so they're grateful.

The Beehive becomes another locked room. French Street darkens, the houses shove closer together, the spindles inside the textile mills whir in your ears as loud as they did on Second Street. Your stepmother never does take that tumble down the stairs. The bees bring you honey each year into the fall.

• • •

In 1892, The Old Man has a spell at the Union Savings Bank, where he's the director. He's lecturing a teller about punctuality, and then he's on the floor being fanned by Mrs. Elbert Gravelock. Dr. Bowen applies mustard plasters to his chest and prescribes brandy, but these are palliatives only. There is no cure for a failing heart.

Miss Kitty Weathercock worries about her father's health. There's still no will saying what will happen to her and her sister, Adeline, after he dies. You see the lawyer again but don't need him to tell you what's next. You already know what the law allows when there's no will, the bulk of an estate passing to the spouse of the deceased and then to the spouse's next of blood kin, who you aren't.

Think of all the times you passed your stepmother's kin in the street, pretending not to hear them say *good morning*. Think of the times you wouldn't come down for tea with the half-sister. *Talk to the hand.* There were always unseen other choices, as there must be now. You think of that old saying, *A stitch in time saves nine.* Mrs. Borden says it when she's tidying the house, doing little tasks to keep everything from falling apart. You didn't know until now that it meant you could go back, undo everything from the past.

*

Go to Lizzie Borden Took an Axe (Pg. 214) or The Farm (Pg. 220)

Lizzie Borden Took an Axe

The song will talk about an axe, but you'll kill them with a hatchet.

Use the hatchet because now that you have your own house, sneakier ways of killing are out. Poison, uncovered wells, ground-up glass in oatmeal, elaborate traps on the stairs. Do it in the middle of the night, when you can't get a witness. Slip in like a thief in the night, like Jesus into a believer's heart. Father hasn't bothered to change the locks.

"Break a window on your way out," Emma doesn't say because she has a raisin and you don't.

When people ask questions, tell them you only unlocked the door for The Thing, who's the real criminal. Tell them what the real crime is.

Your stepmother goes down easy. One whack for the half-sister, one for walking around in your mother's skin, the rest for everything else. There's a moment when you think you'll spare The Old Man, leave it at that, but then his eyes open. In the dark he can't see he's covered in his wife's blood.

"You've come back," he says.

The Thing is the only person you can't fool. It knows why you're here. "People don't kill like this for money," it says.

You know. It knows you know. You know it knows you know that the force working against an object equals mass times the amount a person has suffered. It is the hot locked box you won't get out of any other way. The one eye left in The Old Man's head when it's done follows you around the room.

*
Go to Down a Well (Pg. 215)
or Jump Rope (Pg. 217)
or Dissolution (Pg. 224)

Down a Well

After the trial, take Emma out to the family farm in Swansea to forget. It was one of your favorite places before everything went into the crapper. The Old Man would take you and Emma and old Mrs. Borden to the little Cape Cod house with doors you found out were called *cerulean*, the color you thought whales might be. You stopped going five years ago after a fight with The Old man, but the farm is so beautiful you can't remember what the fight was about. You killed them over it, you remember that much.

Emma says, "Why don't we just stay out here? They'll never find us."

The news reporters find you a few days later. Most of them want the same story, your life as a free woman. The *Boston Herald* reporter skulks around hoping you'll murder someone. The paper was against you during the trial, so he's the one to watch out for. He could sell a story about you drowning puppies, poisoning the groundskeeper. He doesn't have a raisin either.

"Why don't you get a life, loser?" you tell him.

He smiles, flashes a row of long yellow teeth and walks toward you—reason enough to run.

The groundskeeper has left the cover off the well, which is why you don't see the hole in the ground. You're looking behind you to see if the *Herald* reporter is still there, so you don't know there's a hole until you're inside it. It has no bottom. You fall until the opening is a pinprick with voices coming through it. Emma, the reporter, the groundskeeper, who tries to thread a rope down the hole.

"What have I done? I've killed Miss Borden," he says.

He doesn't know the well isn't a hole but a passageway, and that when you come out the other end you're back at the beginning.

*
*Go to Fury (Pg. 179)
or Emma (Pg. 202)*

Jump Rope

The Hamilton girls are out in the street skipping a rope, singing that awful song.

Lizzie Borden took an axe.

You're an old woman now. You pull back the curtains, bothered more by the noise than the words of the song, which has been in your head so long it's like a train going past that you don't hear. Imagine the street is a line of quicksand gobbling the girls. Their noise recedes into the ruckus of Fall River, the milk trucks and the newsboys and someone's clattering Buick negotiating potholes. Cars are motorized now, a sign of the future tunneling out of the present.

Helen, your maid, doesn't know who made up the song. You must have grilled her about it a hundred times, trying to thread it back to its source. She talks to people, so she knows. She says the song has no author, that it's just a thing people say.

"You can't trace these things backwards," she says.

It had to come from somewhere. Children repeat what their parents say. Try to remember the first person who left the courthouse, the prosecutor's words still rattling in their ears.

Lizzie Borden took an axe.

It was a hatchet. How many times do you have to tell people?

The jury's mustaches formed a daisy chain across the courtroom. The fore-stache holding your fate on a slip of paper read *not guilty* because women couldn't be. Not women like you, anyway. You were like this rich girl, one of them. If a Thing could live in your house, it could be living in theirs.

"Where is Emma?" you ask, and Helen pretends not to hear.

Then you remember, you haven't had a letter from Emma since 1912. Somehow she slipped out of sight, out of this house. You'd fought about the people you were running around with then. Half of them are dead now, and Nance O'Neil, the actress who loved you enough to make a movie about you, is an old married woman. You don't speak to her either.

You can look back, see the moment in time where it was still possible for things to be all right and return to it. You want to use the new telephone thingamajig Helen talked you into installing and tell Emma those people are gone with the wind, that she can come back and everything will be as it was, but you haven't figured out how to work it yet.

When the Hamilton girls have gone inside for supper, walk into the street and retrieve their skipping rope.

"The street is not your front parlor," you say, shaking the rope for the parents to see.

They seldom see you. The rare times you talk to people, they look through you as if you are a ghost, seeing the skulls of your father and stepmother split open, brains tumbling out. You don't exist except for the story about you, but they still double bolt their doors. Hoping they're watching, you loop the rope around your neck and hang yourself in the street.

End

The Farm

When your father dies of heart failure, you're forty-seven years old. Emma is even older than that. Your stepmother soldiered on into old age, surviving irritable bowel and a tumor Dr. Bowen had to cut out of her belly. It was why she and your father never had children. The thought that they might have tried upsets your stomach.

Mr. Jennings, The Old Man's lawyer, comes to the house with a file of papers. Not caring about creature comforts, The Old Man had refused to write a will to the end, leaving everything in the hands of the courts. No one in his family would be destitute, he'd insisted. What more did they want?

It takes another ten years for your stepmother to kick. Mrs. Borden humps around the house for the next decade, bumming you out, too stout to climb the stairs. One morning you find her dead in the parlor, which has become her bedroom, her dead eyes like marbles turned to the ceiling.

"No one's going to be out on the street. Just remember that," Mr. Jennings says.

"Destitution is in the eye of the beholder," you say.

There's a long list of things you want. Pots of skin

cream from the pharmacy, hairpins, apricots from the grocery, a cool, airy house to haunt.

You and Emma get to keep the Second Street house, but most of the money and property goes to Mrs. Borden's people. The once impoverished half-sister The Old Man rescued buys a house on The Hill. You walk up there in the middle of the night in your nightgown and think of burning it down with her in it. These days there are a lot of things you want to burn down.

Don't go to Mrs. Borden's funeral. Leave it to the half-sister, who can stand on her new front porch and look down on you, your places reversed. Let people gossip about it. Twenty years ago it mattered what people thought, but life has skipped ahead without you. There's nothing to climb toward anymore.

. . .

A week later, sneak out to the family farm in Swansea to wait. For what, you don't know. It was one of your favorite places when you were young. The Old Man would take you and Emma and old Mrs. Borden, who was doughy inside and out, to the little Cape Cod house with doors you found out were called *cerulean,* the color you thought whales might be. You stopped going fifteen years ago, after some fight with The Old Man, but it's so long ago you can't remember about what the fight was about. You'd wanted to kill them over it, you remember that much.

It takes a month for your stepmother's people to figure out you're here. A businessman in a striped suit who they've hired to inspect all The Old Man's properties finds you weeding pansies in the window boxes, making things nice after all that's happened.

"This is private property, Miss. Don't suppose you know," he says.

When you tell him your name, he recognizes it from the estate papers, one of the poor spinster daughters who lost everything. He says he doesn't want to make things worse for you, but he's got a job to do.

"Miss Borden, please, the property needs appraising. The owners want to sell it."

"I'm the owner," you say, which makes him reach into his breast pocket for something.

You're in the way here, an impediment to someone's happiness. When the man reaches into his coat, he's going for a copy of the deed, the proof you shouldn't be here, but you think he's reaching for a hatchet. You don't know why. Because of that show at the traveling circus when you were a child, the knife thrower who also threw hatchets at his beloved's head? You had to drag Emma to it. You've been thinking about this lately, how you might have changed the course of your own life. Some decisive action, quick as throwing a hatchet. Time is a forward-moving line, created by your choices. Maybe there's nothing you could have done. At any rate, you think he's got a hatchet or something else shiny and sharp in his coat, and it's reason enough to run.

The groundskeeper has taken the well cover off, leaving a hole exposed on the ground. You're looking behind you to see if the man is coming after you, so you don't see the hole until you're inside it. It has no bottom. You fall until the opening is a pinprick with voices coming through it. Emma, the man in the striped suit, the groundskeeper, all fading into a smaller and smaller pinprick, a circle containing the whole world. You're on the outside of it.

End

Dissolution

The men in your house are ghost hunters, people who go around stirring up the past for money. You've seen their television show, *The Spirit Stalker*, because the people who now live in your house watch it. You'd rather watch *Golden Girls*, which is actually about something.

The host's hair is arranged in short spikes on top of his head, and he raises the ghosts by insulting them, hoping to catch a voice on his recording device. At the beginning of each episode, he says the same thing.

"This is... *The Spirit Stalker*."

These days your house is an inn, where people pay to sleep amongst evil spirits. They have their pictures taken while sprawled on the parlor settee with their tongues hanging out like The Old Man or lying face down on the guest room floor like Mrs. Borden. There's even a society dedicated to you. Once a year, the morbidly fascinated gather from across America to reenact the murders, playing the parts of you and Bridget and the Irish policemen, who rifled through your underwear. You guess they rifle through each other's underwear. You're a hundred and twenty years famous.

The host sits on the settee where The Old Man died,

trying for gravitas as he talks into the video camera.

"Tonight *The Spirit Stalker* team takes on one of American history's greatest mysteries. Was Lizzie Borden a murdering psychopath? Did the maid do it? Or was there a more sinister force at work in the Borden house that day... maybe even... paranormal?"

You don't want to be on television. Hide upstairs while the Thing swirls around them in a dark mist, putting kill-thoughts in their heads. Feel regret when the cameraman is swallowed by it and punches his assistant for stepping into the shot. Hear your own scratchy voice on the tape, *Get out*.

The Thing volunteers to get rid of them.

"I don't care for your methods," you say.

"Lizzie Borden took an axe!" the Thing says. "LOL!!"

The Thing wants to turn them against each other. When the owners unlock the front door in the morning, it wants them to find a slaughter: eyeballs and jawbones, a lacework of blood on the walls. It's overambitious. All anybody gets out of "the lockdown," as the idiots call it, is a few spooky sounds on tape, one of them your voice. They play it back so many times it stops sounding like you or like a voice at all.

Months later, you see yourself on television, and it's weird. They keep showing that awful photo of you with the bug eyes that made the set assistant say *She looks wackadoodle*. It puts your life into perspective. They barely mention Emma, like she didn't figure in at all.

After the television show airs, the Thing gets full of itself, thinking it was the star. It becomes difficult to live with.

"I'm gonna show these jerks who runs this joint!" it says.

By now it's an old spirit. It's been haunting for two hundred years, but people aren't as malleable as they used to be, not as willing to believe in things. It hasn't inhabited a body since you. The best it can do is turn over trash cans and slam doors.

"It's disconcerting, more than anything else," the next owner tells the exorcist she hires to cleanse the place. She's decided to run a travel agency out of the downstairs and wants a fresh start. "I feel like someone's always watching me in the shower."

The exorcist focuses on getting the Thing out of the house, not you. He understands this is your house, and whatever you've done he doesn't have the right to kick you out. He hands the Thing a brochure and says,

"Look, buddy, it's time to move on."

The brochure is advertising an assisted living facility called Dr. Balthazar's Home for Aging and Unsettled

Spirits. It's got a gym and a dining hall and a barber shop, all inclusive.

"Who would I terrorize?" the Thing asks.

"The staff, I guess."

"Sweet."

"What about crucifixes and holy water?" you say.

People have brought all that into the house before in hopes of dislodging you, and none of it's worked. You're still here, you and the Thing. The Old Man and Mrs. Borden are here, too.

"That's not really how I roll," the exorcist says.

He's one of those new-wave exorcists who try to reason with dark spirits to get them to see there are other options in the afterlife. So far, he seems legit.

"Whatever, this place is played anyway," the Thing says.

When the Thing moves out, it's just you and the other Bordens. Cousin Eliza appears at the same time every day, wringing her hands over what she's done. Your stepmother is caught in a loop, always heading up the front stairs to change bed linens.

"Going up to tidy the guest room," she says, forty-seven times a day.

The Old Man lies on the settee with his head in his hands.

Spirits can only haunt a place for so long before they lose molecular cohesion. The bonds that have tied them to a place break down, and they forget what they're doing there. Paranormal dementia. Eventually they lose the thread of their lives. It will happen to you, but not soon enough.

Emma has never appeared in the house. You'd thought that at the moment of her death she'd appear here, where everything happened, but she must have become tied to another place. She's mixing with the ghosts of her own life in New Hampshire, which you can't picture because you never visited. It's what, a hundred miles at most? A missed opportunity.

Over the next century, you try and fail to picture Emma in her other house, Emma in life, Emma tidying a shell garden in front of her house, Emma at the beach with sunburned ankles, Emma in death, and finally give in to watching The Old Man and Mrs. Borden fade, their edges melting away until they're just dark smudges occasionally moving around the house. Then you're alone.

End

Dark Paradise

The police are already in the house when you come home, shivering out of your skin. A fog blankets the street. It feels like Halloween, but it's not. The only spook is you waltzing in like you own the place. You do own the place now, but you're not supposed to know this yet.

The police captain asks where you've been. "Too thick for decent people to be out," he says. He needn't worry. You only went to the pharmacy for stomach pills because everyone's been sick. Also, you aren't decent. You speak in present tense to show you don't know about the bodies in the parlor, hidden under sheets.

"What's the meaning of this? Where are my father and stepmother?" you ask. "They need their medicine."

He regrets to inform you.

By the time The Old Man and your stepmother are loaded into a carriage, it's storming out. It's just you and the police captain. The way the scene is written, you know you're supposed to do something called swooning, *and he's supposed to feel sympathy for you because this just, well . . . who can believe it? You're like this rich girl.*

"You couldn't have been involved in this," he says. "I feel as if I've known you forever."

"That doesn't mean I couldn't be involved in this," you say.

A flash of lightning turns everything silver, and an organ chord pulsates. This must be how people talk when they're falling in love.

The captain's name is Frank Swanson. He looks like a boy you liked in school, whose name you can't remember. You tell him he reminds you of a boy who could quote the Second Law of Thermodynamics and stuttered the first words of sentences, and he smiles like you've said a romantic thing. It's the point in the story where you're supposed to give something up. Part of yourself: body, thoughts, facts that will incriminate you. If you do it for love, it will be worth it. Struggle a little to not appear willing, hate yourself later. Allow yourself to be double-crossed. During the next lightning strike, the electric goes out and the dark seems to have arms and legs wrapping around you.

• • •

Swanson's hot but dumber than a bag of socks. He would make you go soft if you had soft places. By the time the pharmacist rats you out for trying to buy poison (you tried that first, landing you with a houseful of sick stomachs to tend), Swanson's already in love with you.

Another storm is kicking up outside. Run out into it. It's the natural thing to do when there's this much to run from. Run into the storm to forget, to seem distraught, weak and crazy. Swanson will chase you down the street like when you were a girl and the Thing came into your room and you ran out into the night, thinking you were safer outside the house. He doesn't know about the Thing or your hollow center or any of the forces in your life that have converged to run you out into a thunderstorm, except that you've murdered your parents. He thinks you're running out of guilt. Maybe he's pinned some kind of hope to it, like they won't be able to prove you did it or there's some good reason—you could give him dozens: the heat in the house that day, the ineffectiveness of poison, the sour breath of the Thing in your ear telling you to do it.

"Tell me they abused you," he yells into the storm.

They had, in one way or another, even your stepmother, who was doughy inside and out. She had to walk out of rooms to forget.

"Tell me you went temporarily insane."

What strange things to want for the person you love.

. . .

You've reached the beach. Inexplicably, there's a beach at the end of your street, flashing purple with each crack of lightning, being torn up by the thundercloud spiraling above it. Women should always run away from their lovers in thunderstorms to organ music. How else would they know their lives had reached some kind of climax?

"Millie, stop," Swanson yells. "Millie Gordon."

You invented him as a girl, wanting to be liked by a boy who knew how electromagnetism works. He seemed real enough in your bed and seems real enough now, a warm body pulling you closer with the force of its gravity. When he finally catches you, you're up to your knees in the water, your skirt blousing around you like a Portuguese man o' war.

You say, "I am a Portuguese man o' war." You worry your skin will touch his and electrocute him.

The water is what tells you it's a dream. There isn't any water this close to the house. You and your sister Gemma used to build sandcastles on Horseneck Beach big enough to get inside and pretend you lived in them. Instead of a beach at the end of your street, there's the cemetery where your parents were buried yesterday. You used to pretend the headstones were houses. You were always pretending with houses. The ones you lived in, the ones you stole, the ones that had to be made up.

"The water makes this a dream," you say.

When Swanson enters the water, you know he's coming in to drown you. The rain has stopped. There's just the purple thundercloud hanging over the water as it retreats out to sea, leaving a purple sky lit up by a purple moon.

"I'm an officer of the law," he says. Something about duty. You can't hear clearly over the waves.

Where is Gemma? The morning of the murders she asked you not to do anything you couldn't undo. She knows how your mind works. She knows to watch for the void expanding inside you. She can't see it, but she knows its shape. There's a look on your face she calls The Cloud for its darkness, and because the hole inside you is an unstable emptiness it collapses, and then people's things go missing, then they're dead. Gemma, the only person you love, must have run away when she saw what you'd done.

When he pushes you under the black water, you wonder if it's possible to die in a dream and not wake up in the real world, if that's what happens when people die in their sleep. You think you must have died this way before.

* *End*

Acknowledgements

The author wishes to the thank the following publications for giving stories in this collection their first homes:

> *The Conium Review*
> *Fiddleblack*
> *Literary Orphans*
> *Paper Darts*
> *The Rumpus*
> *Shirley*

About the Author

Emily Koon is a fiction writer from North Carolina. She has work in *Atticus Review*, *Necessary Fiction*, *Paper Darts*, *Portland Review*, *The Rumpus*, and other places.

This book was selected by Matt Bell as winner of the Conium Press Book & Chapbook Contest. Emily previously won *The Conium Review*'s 2015 Innovative Short Fiction Contest, judged by Amelia Gray.